The Matter of the Duct Tape Tuxedo

AND OTHER IMPOSSIBLE CRIME SHORT STORIES

Captain Heinz Noonan,
the Bearded Holmes: Book One

ISBN Number: 978-1-59433-862-5
eBook ISBN Number: 978-1-59433-863-2
Library of Congress Catalog Card Number: 2019942430

—First Edition—

Manufactured in the United States of America

"Just when I think I've heard it all
I get another phone call."

. . . *Heinz Noonan*

THE MATTER OF THE DUCT TAPE TUXEDO

Captain Noonan, the "Bearded Holmes" of the Sandersonville, North Carolina Police Department, was barely conscious of the strange presence in his office until a high-pitched male voice said, "Excuse me."

Noonan looked up – "up" being the operative word – and saw no one. He saw no one, the detective realized, until he noticed the top of a bald head just at the foot of his field of view. Adjusting his gaze downward, he found himself looking at a perfect man, just downsized, whose head barely protruded above the level of the desk.

"May I help you?" Noonan asked, a bit nervous to be looking at the man half his size, he, Noonan, being seated and the midget fully erect.

"Don't let my size fool you," said the little man. "I have a Ph. D. in mathematics and a black belt in Tae Kwon Do. No, I don't pick on mosquitoes, smoking did not stunt my growth and my wife is not a giant, just full size, the American average of five foot eight. And," his eyes flashed, "we've been married for 12 years and have two children, both normal from your point of view."

"We're a little testy this morning, aren't we?" Noonan asked with a wry smile.

"When you're my size you've heard all the jokes," the little man said. "So I try to get the derogatory statements out of the way quickly. Everyone thinks they're a comic when it comes to midgets. I am a midget, by the way, not a dwarf. A dwarf is misshapen. A midget . . ."

"That I know," said Noonan humorously. "A midget is a relative."

"Sorry?"

"That's a family joke," Noonan said as he smiled. "My brother is married to a woman whose family name is Midyette. It's French."

"For midget?"

"Maybe. But they are a family of short people. Not midgets. Just short. So it's a family joke, mixing Midyette with midget."

"I'll bet they don't think it's funny?"

"Actually, they're in real estate so anything that helps the client remember their name is fine with them. Can you imagine that? A whole family of realtors in a town on the Outer Banks that is so small it doesn't have mail delivery?"

"That's keeping it in the family."

"Everyone *in* the hamlet is family." Noonan smiled. "Now that I know you don't fight mosquitoes or have trouble with the mathematics puzzlers, may I be so bold as to ask why you're here?"

"You won't believe this but . . ."

"Let me tell you something before you start. The strangest cases in America come through that door," Noonan said as he pointed at his office doorway. "I've had everything from kidnapped alligators to corpses making obscene phone calls. I don't think you can surprise me."

"OK. In that case, I need help in finding the Komodo dragon trousers from my duct tape tuxedo."

"I spoke too soon," Noonan said as he shook his head. "I'm not sure I do believe you."

"I thought you might find it hard to believe so I brought a photograph." The midget handed Noonan a photograph that was the size of his, the midget's, head. It was an 8-by-10 of the midget in a strange outfit that may very well have included Komodo dragon trousers. He was standing next to a woman whose head was out of the photograph. "This is a shot of me and my wife – or at least part of my wife – taken last year."

"And these, I take it, are the Komodo dragon trousers?" Noonan pointed at the trousers in the photograph.

"Yes. But that is not the duct tape tuxedo."

"My wife is Alaskan so I know what duct tape is. Can I assume that a duct tape tuxedo is a tuxedo make of duct tape?"

"You can but you'd be wrong. In this case, the tuxedo is made from the duct tape fabric but without the glue. I had the tuxedo specially made for novelty occasions. I have," he smiled thinly, "quite an ability to raise money for charities. The audience expects something different so I oblige them. A duct tape tuxedo is different and lasts longer than a normal suit."

"I see. And the Komodo dragon trousers?"

"Actually they are called Komodo trousers because they appear to be made from a Komodo dragon's skin. Actually they are snake skin of some kind. From Mexico. I wear the Komodo trousers when there is no food involved. I'd hate to stain them."

"What kind of charities to you attend?"

"Any kind that involve children, disabled people or hospices. I don't 'attend' them; I appear as a celebrity and help them raise money. I don't charge for my services."

"I see," Noonan hesitated. "I hate to ask this, but is your celebrity because of your size of something else?"

"I worked my way through college as a circus midget." Noonan started to say something but the man cut him off. "Everyone has had a part time job. That was mine. It was kind of a natural. The money was good, I like to travel and I went to school during the cold months. It took me 15 years to get through college and graduate school. When I quit the circus I swore I would never be in a freak show again. Then my oldest child got diabetes and I started helping the American Diabetes Foundation raise money for research. It worked so well that I kept up the appearances."

"You son is all right now?"

"He's holding his own, watching his diet. He'll be OK. Thanks for asking."

"OK. Tell me about the missing trousers."

"I came all the way to meet you in person because I didn't think you'd believe me over the phone. All evidence indicates that the trousers were stolen by a Big Foot."

"Big Foot? You mean like a *Sasquatch*? This is North Carolina, not the Pacific Northwest."

"Yup. And the local police were laughing so hard they didn't hear the rest of the story."

"Where, might I ask, do you live?"

"Just outside of Charlotte. In a small town. You wouldn't know the name."

"Do you have a lot of Big Foot robberies out there?"

"Is that supposed to be funny?"

"No. This is serious. If you are serious. Any other robberies that have been linked to this *Sasquatch*?"

"Can it be proven, no. Are there suspicious burglaries that are similar to mine, yes. About six."

"Tell me about your robbery and then the other ones."

"OK." The midget reached into his pocket and pulled out a business card which he handed up and across the desk top to Noonan.

"The Gnarly Gnome?" Noonan said and then looked up from the card.

The midget smiled and shrugged his shoulders. "Everyone's got to have a stage name. Actually, it's the 'Gnarly Gnome from Nome.' The 'from Nome' part is not on the card. It was alliterative and anyone will believe anything about Alaska in the Lower 48."

"I know," Noonan said. "My wife is Alaskan."

"Which is why I'm here, frankly. I wanted this case to be taken seriously."

"So far all I know is that you suspect a *Sasquatch* of stealing a pair of green Mexican snakeskin pants that are part of a duct tape tuxedo you use when you make appearances as the Gnarly Gnome from Nome. Sounds like a simple case. You just find the *Sasquatch* and you've got the pants."

"Trousers. *Pants* are like jeans. *Trousers* are dressy. You throw your pants on a chair after wearing them all day. You wear your trousers for dress occasions and hang them up neatly when you get home."

"I stand corrected. And, yes, I do take you seriously. Let's talk about your robbery."

"I'm glad *someone* is finally taking me seriously. Our family lives outside of Sydneyville about sixty miles from Charlotte. We're in the forest in the sense that we don't have nearby neighbors. Sydneyville is rural anyway so being out of town means your next-door neighbor is five miles away. There's not a lot of crime in Sydneyville; less and less the farther we get away from the town center. We've had some poaching on our land and someone set a fire by accident but that's about it."

"How much land do you own?"

"None. The bank owns all of it. We're buying it."

"OK. How many acres are you buying from the bank?"

"Ten acres, more or less. There's a lot of national and state park land around us so we're almost in-holders. All of our roads are in so we aren't having any trouble with regulators."

"Do you work at home?"

"No. In Sydneyville. I'm a CPA."

"With a Ph. D. in Mathematics?"

"I worked with NASA for a while. Got tired of Florida. Too many strange people. My wife's from Charlotte so we moved back to North Carolina."

"Does your wife work in town?"

"With me. Yes. Both kids go to school in town. We all drive in together so the house is empty all day."

"And the robbery?"

"We came home three weeks ago and found the back door broken in. There was a lot of hair on the broken glass and frame and muddy footprints on the rug. Big feet. They kind of wandered through the house, ended up in the bedroom where the trousers were on the bed. I was going to be doing a charity appearance for the Sydneyville Blue Ridge Hospice Tag Team Race the night the pants disappeared."

"The pants were stolen?"

"Yeah."

"Anything else?"

"I'm not sure. A lot of stuff was knocked over and scattered. Not like someone was dumping drawers looking for money or anything like that. More like the kitchen table overturned and the salt and pepper shakers bouncing all over the floor with napkin rings and a coffee cup full of spoons."

"But nothing else was missing?"

"I have a list of suspected items that are missing but I'm not absolutely sure that all are missing or that there are other small items missing that I don't know about yet."

"Let's see the list."

The Gnarly Gnome handed Noonan a list which the detective poured over, tilting his head back for the best use of his bifocals. He read the items off one at a time.

"Plastic handled bread knife."

"I got it one summer in Paris, France. While I was with a circus. The lederhosen are from Germany. Same summer."

Noonan looked down the list. "*Lederhosen.* Those are the short leather pants, right?"

"Yes. And very small and very worn. They are even too small for my boys.

"Those would be hard to pawn," Noonan smiled. "Were the *lederhosen* out or in a closet?"

"I don't know. I just know they are gone. Like I said, the list is an odd one."

"Where are the *lederhosen* usually?"

"On a shelf in the closet."

"Do they smell?"

"N-o-o-o-o, not that I know of. I can't smell them. Why?"

"Well, I find it hard to believe that the Big Foot would paw through a closet looking for something specific that didn't have a smell."

"There are leather jackets in that closet so if the *lederhosen* smelled, so did the other leather jackets."

"Humm. Noonan kept going down the list. "One sandal, opened bag of flour . . .

"Opened," said the Gnome, "as in torn open. Not stolen, just torn open."

"Any flour missing?"

"We don't know. It was spilled and there were footprints in it. If any was stolen there's no way to know."

"I see." Noonan kept reading. "pair of reading glasses, and a handful of grapes."

"I'm pretty sure whoever was there was eating the grapes. I mean, why steal them?"

Noonan nodded. "You are right. It is an odd list. But these are the items that were stolen, right?"

"Well," the Gnome paused, "it depends on what you mean by 'stolen.' If you mean spirited, away, yeah."

"Do you have another definition?"

"Well, I wouldn't call the flour stolen."

Noonan thought for a moment. "That's true. *Damaged* would be a better term. I guess I'd call the grapes *damaged* as well since they probably weren't stolen in the traditional sense of the word."

"That's right," said the Gnome.

"Well, what else was *damaged* but not stolen?"

That caught the Gnome by surprise. "That would be difficult to say. I mean, we filled out the Police Report with what was stolen. The damages for the insurance company were in the cumulative. That is, the insurance wanted to know how much damage was done in the dollar sense. The dollars weren't high because there was no structural damage. So it was just the replacement of the stolen property, repair of the property that was damaged and a generic list of the damaged property that was not repairable."

Noonan rolled the list of stolen property into a tube. "OK. What was damaged that could not be repaired?"

"Well," the Gnome scratched his head. "There was the flour of course. Then there was some damage in the office. The desk mat was ripped apart, the desk calendar had its pages ripped out and tossed around, there were a handful of pens that were stepped on and broken and a painting was jerked off a wall with its frame broken." The small man scratched his head as he thought. "There was also a broken flashlight. I keep a flashlight on the shelf behind my desk just in case the electricity goes out," the Gnome added. "In the bedroom the sheets were pretty badly ripped and the stuff was pulled down out of the closet. That's all I can think of. That's all the stuff, repairable and not repairable."

"Humm," Noonan thought for a moment. "You said there were other, similar robberies."

"If you mean do the police call them *robberies,* no. They call them pranks."

"Same kind of damage?"

"Pretty much the same. Someone broke in, ran amuck, caused damage and left."

"Was anything actually stolen in those incidents?

"Nothing big. Maybe some shiny things. Not much else."

"But there was damage in other robberies – assuming we can call them robberies."

"As far as I know. What the police said was that over the past six or seven weeks there had been about six break-ins with nothing of value stolen. That's what they said. I didn't check it out."

Noonan scratched his forehead with the paper tube he had made of the list of stolen items. He was silent for a moment and then he re-looked at the list. Finally he said, "Can I assume that the bread knife was in the kitchen?"

"Actually it was on the desk. I use it as a letter opener."

"And the reading glasses?"

"One the desk as well."

"Tell me about the layout of your house starting with the door that was broken in."

"The door that was broken in was the kitchen door," said the Gnarly Gnome from Nome. "The intruder apparently went around in the kitchen and then went into the office. After trashing the office he, she, it, whatever went into the master bedroom that is off the office. That's where the pants were stolen."

"Is there a living room off the master bedroom?"

"Yes. Under normal circumstances you'd come in front door into what we call the 'Great Room.' There's a bathroom off to one side and the other two bedrooms are upstairs."

"But the intruder only went through kitchen, office and master bedroom."

"That's right."

"What kind of damage was done in the master bedroom?"

"None. Just the stolen trousers."

"Was there any sign that the intruder went into the Great Room or the other rooms?"

"No. Just the opposite. He, she, it ripped open the flour so the footprints were visible and only in the kitchen, office and bedroom. Then whatever it was went out the broken door."

"I'm going to assume that the footprints were kind of random until they got to the master bedroom and then went straight out the back door."

The Gnome shook his head in disbelief. "How did you know that?"

Noonan smiled. "Because sometimes I am a clever man. OK, here's what I want you to do for me. First, look for the *lederhosen* in the house. They have not been stolen, just misplaced."

"How do you know that?"

"For the moment, trust me."

"OK."

"I need a complete list of everything that was on the desk, no matter how trivial."

"OK."

"As far as the other robberies are concerned, I need to know what was stolen and what was missing at each of the other robberies. I also need to know if flour or any other substance was involved that showed footprints. You'll have to call each one of the homes and ask them to give you a list of what was damaged and if there was anything else that missing no matter how trivial."

"Is that all?"

"No, as a matter of fact. I will also need the location of each home in the sense that I want to know what is around them. Are they secluded or in neighborhoods? Are they clustered in one neighborhood or scattered around? What door was used by the intruder in each case? Were only kitchens, offices and bedrooms rummaged? What is the family make-up of each of the homes that were entered, where do the parents work, if there are children where do they go to school and when are the children supposed to be at their particular schools. . . ."

"Just a second," said the Gnome. "I'm writing as fast as I can and I am way behind you."

Noonan smiled and sat silently until the Gnome stopped writing. "Anything else?"

"Just one more thing. You said you were going to be wearing your pants the night they were stolen."

"That's correct."

"What was the name of the nonprofit you were going to raise money for?"

"The Sydneyville Blue Ridge Hospice Tag Team Race."

"OK. See if you can find a list of people who were supposed to be there that night."

"Supposed to be or were there?"

"Supposed to be. I'm assuming that they sold tickets of some kind but not everyone showed up for the event. Sometimes companies buy a block of tickets and then give them one at a time to clients or friends or donate them to another charitable cause, right?"

"We sold about 300 tickets and had about 100 people show up but there is no way to tell who those people were."

"I'm not concerned about who actually showed up, just who bought the tickets."

"That's going to be rough. A bank might buy ten tickets so all you will know is that the bank bought ten tickets."

"That'll have to be good enough."

The Gnome gave Noonan a pleasant look. "You are really taking this seriously."

"Just get me that information and then we'll see about getting those pants back."

It took two days for the midget to get back to Noonan. But he was still not sure the detective had been serious.

"You were serious, right?"

"As serious as I can be. I can't solve every matter than comes across my desk but I try mightily for each one."

"That's good enough for me. In what order do you want the information?"

"Doesn't matter. Go ahead."

"All right," and Noonan could hear papers being shuffled. "What was on my desk the day of the break-in was a cup of pens, a dictionary, blank pad of paper, small wooden bear, reading glasses, lamp, rolodex, desk calendar, desk blotter, scotch tape dispenser, a small scale to weigh letters, stamps in a small metal box, stapler, a pile of envelopes and a paperweight in the form of an apple."

"But the only things amiss were the missing reading glasses, the damaged desk blotter and the torn apart desk calendar, correct?"

"That's right."

"Was the desk calendar a book with a spine or a notebook, maybe with a spiral binding?"

"I have both. The book with a spine is for personal items and I keep it in the desk. The day-to-day is loose-leaf and that was the one that was on the desk and destroyed."

"Were any pages missing?"

"No way to know. It was ripped up so badly I just tossed it. I use it to log down appointments. That's all it had in it."

"OK," said Noonan, "go on."

"Do you want to tell you what was stolen robbery by robbery or just a list?"

"Let's go with the list first."

"Ok, but the list is long and strange."

"I'll bet. Go ahead."

"Two letter openers, can of peas, half-filled bottle of ink, pile of empty cassette mailers, towel, six wooden hangers, package of peanuts, some porcelain figurines, two couch pillows, a plastic cup, a teddy bear and a pair of head phones."

"OK."

"Are you writing these down?"

"No, I'm just listening for the moment. Go on."

"I called all of the homes and asked if anything had been stolen that was not reported and what had been damaged. They all said they had discovered some smaller things missing afterwards but it had not been worth their time to call the police. Those items included an olive fork, cardboard salt-and-pepper shaker set the kind you can buy in the grocery store for about a dollar, three or four oranges, can of anchovies and a box of hair color for men."

"How about the damage?"

"Pretty much the same as my house. Paintings or artwork had been pulled off the wall, desk tops had been swept clear and paperwork scattered."

"Were any of the areas that were attacked offices?"

"Yes and no. In two of the six homes there were stand-alone offices and they were ravaged. In the other four the desk was in a bed room or along a living room wall so you could not call the rooms an office. But all of the desks had damage. Mostly it was scattering documents and ripped up papers."

"What kinds of things were ripped apart on the desks?"

"It was hard to tell. Everyone had the same problem I did. They saved the important papers and everything else got dumped. That included some desk calendars and date books, a college class notebook, a loose-leaf collection of poetry, some Manila file folders with bills and some check stubs."

"Nothing else?"

"Nothing that anyone can remember."

"Ok. Go on."

"As far as the location of the homes, they are all within the city limits and not that far from one another. But that's not saying much because all of the homes in Sydneyville are fairly close to one another. It's a small town. Two of them are in a traditional neighborhood and have fences. Whoever burgled those homes had to get over the fence. The other four do not have fences. Other than my house, only one is what I could call secluded. The intruder entered a back door in all homes. Five of six back doors actually went into a kitchen and the sixth went into a door that was next to a kitchen. All of the homes had the kitchen, office or office areas and at least one bedroom ravaged.

There is no evidence that any other rooms were entered. All of the homes have children and all the children go to the same schools. But this is not uncommon because, . . ."

"I know," said Noonan. "It's a small town."

"You are correct," said the midget. "All children are at school by 8 a.m. and home no earlier than 2:45 in the afternoon. Only my home had footprints and no other home had any damage to the kitchen that would have led to footprints being found."

"How about the people who owned the homes. Do you know any other them?"

"Actually, yes. But they again . . ."

"Sydneyville is a small place, right?"

"That's right. Of the 12 husbands and wives, three are clients themselves and another four worked for clients that my firm services. The rest worked in businesses ranging from a grocery store to a gas station to a hair salon."

"OK. Now, how about those charity tickets. Did you get a list of the people who bought them?"

"Yes, but I don't know. . ."

"You never know what you will find. Did any of the people who were burgled buy tickets?"

"Two or three individually, yes. Then all my client companies bought tickets but I don't know to whom they gave the tickets."

"Are any of your client companies in the top five ticket buyers?"

"One. It's the Sydneyville Bank and Trust. They bought 30 tickets."

"Was that a large sale?"

"Biggest. The next one down is 10 tickets."

"Other than the couple that's associated with the Bank and Trust, do any of the other home owners have anything to do with the bank – other than they do business there?"

"Well, yes, because it's the only bank in town. Everyone does business there. We have a large hotel and golf course going in and some of the locals have been buying shares through the bank. It formed kind of an investment club to coordinate the dollars."

"Tell me about that investment club."

"It was started by the Sydneyville Bank and Trust to help an out-of-state company fund a hotel and golf course. Land is cheap in Sydneyville and we are just close enough to Charlotte to attract some big city golfers who'd rather spend the weekend golfing in Sydneyville that fight for start time in the bigger city."

"And take their secretaries with them," said Noonan slyly.

"I'd say so," replied the midget. "As long as it's good for business."

"How have investments being going?"

"Pretty good. We formed a corporation and bought up the land that the hotel and golf course would need and transferred it to the out-of-state company in exchange for stock shares. Now we are waiting for the OK from the SEC or whoever approves stuff like that."

"Well," said Noonan sadly, "I hate to tell you this but you've been snookered. That hotel and golf course have been a scam to get the land at no cost. Here's what I think happened. Someone approached the Sydneyville Bank and Trust to help with this so-called hotel and golf course. The bank bent over backwards and used its good name to get investors. But the bank did not do its homework until too late. Only then did it realize that the out-of-state company was a front. Once the title to the land was transferred to the front, it would collapse. Ownership of the land would then be an asset to a deceased company and bought for pennies on the dollar. Some large company was going to end up with the land and the investors will get nothing."

"You're kidding! A lot of money went into that project!"

"I'll bet it did. Too late someone from the bank figured out what was going to happen. The only way it could prevent itself from getting sued was to remove all evidence of its involvement as anything other than a facilitator. Jiggling the records they had was not hard . . ."

"They had a fire in their offices about ten days ago."

"Well," said Noonan sadly. "I'll bet you will find that the fire was in the records room. That will make suing the bank hard. The other records they had to get rid of were the people with whom they had made personal contact. I'm sure you will find that there were six couples, you included. There were no robberies. Everything that was taken was simply to throw the police off the scent. What the burglars really wanted was to destroy all of the calendars, the proof that those six couples had actually met with bank officials. With no proof any meetings had taken place there could be no law suit. The burglars ravaged the homes, stole a few trinkets and then made sure to tear out the pages in the desk diaries and calendars that related to the meetings. Then they ripped the diaries and calendars apart so well that everyone just dumped them. No one knew they were dumping evidence. They figured it was just kids gone wild."

"We've been snookered? Are you sure?"

"I can only guess based on the evidence. But, yes, I think the burglaries were all part of a cover-up scheme by the bank. And I think the bank bought the 30 tickets to the charity event and passed them out as a widely as possible to dispel any suspicion that they were involved."

"But why steal my Komodo pants?"

"You were the most important person to mislead. You're a numbers man. Of all people in town – and it is a small town – you would have smelled something wrong. But you would have only been on the scent if you weren't being distracted by something else. That 'something else' was the pair of trousers. They are your trademark, am I right?"

"That's correct. I'm been stewing about those pants for weeks."

"Then the burglar did his job well. You've been so angry about the pants you have not been 100% at work."

"Unfortunately that is correct."

"I'll bet you will find the trousers and all of the other stuff that was stolen somewhere in the bank. Whoever took the items can't afford to throw them away in town so he – or she – is keeping them for when he – or she – leaves. I'll bet you will find that someone high on the food chain in the bank is planning a trip or a retirement vacation."

"As a matter of fact . . ."

"Well, get to their office before they go. That's where your trousers are. But I'm afraid your money is long gone."

There was a long moment of silence. Finally the midget said, "Unfortunately you may be correct. I'll get right on this. Thank you for your help and do I owe. . . "

"I'm a public servant. You don't owe me anything."

"Well, at the very least, thanks," and that's all the midget said. But an hour later he called back, "just one more quick question."

"The *lederhosen*, right?"

"How did you know that?"

"I'm only half as dumb as I look. Your wife threw them out. She can't stand them. Never could. When the robbery came up it was her moment to give them the deep six. They're probably at the bottom of the Sydneyville land fill under a few tons of garbage."

THE MATTER OF LOUIE THE LOBSTER

Captain Heinz Noonan, the "Bearded Holmes" of the Sandersonville Police Department, was contemplating a meal without the family, a once-a-month blessing when he got to cook his own meal. But, since he knew as much about cooking as he did Tibetan Monk Tantric Harmonics, he left the cooking to someone who knew what he was doing. Or, in this case, she. She, in this case, was Avalon Lone – spelled with a silent "e" she was always quick to say – at the Pamlico Lobster Pit.

Lone was always quick with the joke. She swore she got her lobsters from a pit she dug in her back yard and advised Noonan to dig the same in his back yard. Noonan said he'd love to – right next to his wife's lemon tree so the lobster could eat the lemons and he would not have to season the claws. The two had tried to engage in a pun battle of lobster but, as both discovered, there were not that many lobster jokes and those that were, were not funny. Only two were half-funny: lobsters don't share because they are shellfish and the difference between a decrepit bus station and a lobster with breast implants was that one is a crusty bus station and the other is a busty crustacean.

Lone – with a silent "e" – had been waiting for Noonan for a month for her latest. When the captain came in she said, "You do want a red lobster tail for $5?"

This took the captain by surprise. "A red lobster tail for $5. OK, I'll bite. Yeah."

Lone leaned toward the captain and said, "Once upon a time there was this red lobster who . . ." and then burst into laughter.

"It doesn't come with sauce?" Noonan asked innocently and they both laughed.

When they finished their monthly guffaw, Lone (with the silent "e") pulled Noonan aside and said seriously, "We've had an issue here lately and, frankly, I've been waiting for you to show up."

"An *issue.* Sounds serious."

"Not for me. For Louie."

Louie was Louie the Lobster, the namesake of the Pamlico Lobster Pit. Louie had been pulled from the briny deep and, at the time, was the largest lobster to come out of the Outer Banks lobster bed. He had since been surpassed in weight since then but he was still alive while the other large lobsters had become human bone and tissue. So he was Louie the Lobster, largest living crustacean between Virginia Beach and Ocracoke – and 100 miles inland because there were no lobsters coming out of any part or tributary of Pamlico Sound.

"What's Louie's problem?"

"It's not his problem. It's mine."

"What's your problem with Louie?"

"He's rich. He laid a $25,000 diamond ring."

"That's rich, I must say," said Noonan. "In more ways than one. He laid a diamond ring?"

"Had to have laid it. He's in a cage by himself and the top is locked down."

"You mean the big salt water aquarium with the rocks and kelp where Louie lives?"

"Same one."

"How did Louie say he got the ring?"

"That's what I need you to find out. We clean the cage once a year or so, take Louie out and give the glass a sanitary scrub. Then Louie goes back in with fresh salt water."

"Where's the diamond ring come in?"

"We found it inside the aquarium. Among the rocks."

"Someone probably dropped it in. Hid it maybe. You do feed Louie so the top has to come open once or twice a day."

"True. But we keep the lid locked the rest of the time. We had someone try to steal Louie a few years ago and since then we keep the lid under lock and key. Louie has the lock and I have the key."

"So the aquarium has been under guard the whole time. How do you know the ring is worth $25,000?"

"I took it to an appraiser. I also asked him if it had been stolen. He told me to see the fuzz."

"Fuzz?"

"I'm an old hippy. He's an old hippy. For us it's the fuzz."

"What did the *fuzz* say?"

"No reports of any such ring being stolen. He said I had to put an advertisement in the paper. I did. I got a zillion responses."

"Let me guess, everyone was missing all kinds of jewelry but no request matched the ring."

"Correct."

"So what's the problem? You found the ring. You did your due diligence. Enjoy your lost and found."

"But how did the ring get into Louie the Lobster's aquarium in the first place?"

"Why do you care?"

"Because if someone can put a ring in a locked aquarium they can put in poison. I'd lose Louie and he's my Number One draw."

"I thought it was your food."

"That too. I just want to make sure Louie's safe. Even more important. I'm betting the ring is stolen and the person who owns it doesn't know it's missing yet. I'm also worried that whoever put the ring into the aquarium will be coming back for it. If he can't get it out easily he's likely to break the aquarium. Then there goes Louie."

"Well, let me take a look at the aquarium."

"This is your lock?" Noonan said in astonishment when he saw the salt water fish tank. "This is a padlock! A second-rate burglar could open this up with a pick as fast as you can open it with a key."

"Well! It's the best that I could do!"

Noonan tapped on the aquarium. "In our office lingo, this is a crackerjack box. Having that lock does not mean anything. Anybody could have jimmied it open."

"OK. Maybe. But someone put the ring in the tank."

Lt. Blakely was the best-looking man on the Sandersonville Police Force. He was a blend of every ethnic group on the planet, stood a few inches over six feet, was a marathon runner, weight lifter, had an MBA from Stanford and lived in Sandersonville because his father had Alzheimer's and his mother needed the extra income to take care of the ailing man. He was also single which made a very big difference to the women of Sandersonville, Harperville, Marvin City, Harrisonburg and every other community on the North Carolina coastline that he visited on official business.

"You wanted to see me, chief?" Blakely said to Noonan when he came in from his peripatetic duties.

"Like fish?" Noonan was never good on niceties.

"Catching or eating?"

"Watching."

Blakely was silent for a moment. "I can't say I've ever watched fish. Is this some kind of a joke?"

"Maybe. I have a special assignment for you. It's a casual assignment in the sense that it's something you should be doing while you are out and around."

"As in out and around on duty?"

"Whenever and wherever."

"OK," he paused for a moment and then said, "Is this a trick question?"

"Yes and no."

"I don't like answers like that."

"I know how you feel. Here's the problem. A valuable object appeared in a fish tank. No one knows how it got there. It could have been dropped in. It could have been left by aliens. I don't know. But the one thing I do know is that whoever did the dropping does not live in Sandersonville."

"How do you know that?"

"I'm psychic."

"I can live with that. And you want me to . . ." Blakely let the sentence hang.

"While you are perambulating up and down the coastline, stop in at a few pet stores and see if anything strange has occurred. See what's cooking in the fish business. Actually, *cooking* is not the right verb. How about what is *happening* in the fish business?"

"Yes, sir. And it's a gerund."

"What is?"

"*Cooking*. It's a gerund, not a verb."

Noonan chuckled. "Don't you have something to do?"

"Yes, sir. I'm shuffling on out. That's another . . ."

"Gerund. I know."

Eight days later Noonan got a call back from Blakely.

"I know why you sent me on this assignment, chief."

"Really," Noonan feigned ignorance. "Why is that?"

"There's a North Carolina Pet Association that is very active. And I mean very active. As a matter of fact it was having its annual convention in Harperville. But I guess you didn't know that."

"Really?" Noonan yawned. "Isn't that interesting."

"Yeah," snapped Blakely over the electronic phone lines that did not exit. "I'll also bet you didn't know that pet store owners are about 99% female."

"Really?" Noonan shook his head. "I didn't know that."

"Yes, sir. When people told me you were devious I wasn't sure what they meant. Now I know."

"Really? How interesting. Did you find anything of importance?"

"Of importance, I don't know. But you asked for strange occurrences and robberies. Strange occurrences, yes. Every pet store owner has a dozen. Most of them involve exotic pets I have never heard of. Robberies, a few but hardly unusual. There was a rash of pet food hijackings. I had no idea pet food had that kind of a markup, by the way. A couple of cases of yet-to-be assembled aquariums were broken and about 20 pounds of the stuff you put in aquariums was smashed and scattered. There was an absolute rash of duck breast strip and chicken breast strip robberies. It was odd because the packages were opened. That meant the contents could not be sold so the strips were given to the local ASPCA. Other than that there was a lot of shoplifting of small stuff like fish food containers, flea powder and I know you will not believe this, ratsicles."

"What's a ratsicle?"

"It's a frozen rat. The whole rat. Frozen solid."

"What do you do with a ratsicle?"

"Apparently pet pythons love them."

"Where were these robberies? Particularly the duck and chicken breast strip and the yet-to-be assembly aquariums."

"Yaupon City. Just like the . . ."

"I know what Yaupon is. When did the thefts occur? At the same time or months apart?"

"About a week apart. Last April. Let me see." Noonan could hear what sounded like pages of a notebook being shuffled. Then Blakely was back on the line. "April 10th for the aquarium robbery. Eight months ago. It was discovered fairly quickly. The duck and chicken breast break-in was discovered on the 15th. It was discovered then so the actual damage would have been done earlier."

"Good work, Blakely. Go get lucky."

"Sir, what do aquarium parts and exposed duck strips have to do with anything in Sandersonville?"

"That, lt., is a very interesting question."

If there was any one thing Noonan knew to be true it was that history was a tool. The roots of the future are deeply rooted in the past and the present did not exist. Present was only a description of the instant when the past becomes the future. He knew that if he wanted a see into the future, he had to look backwards. And the best place to look backwards was in the microfilm room of the Sandersonville Public Library.

He went to the microfilm drawer and pulled out the month of April of the *Yaupon City Gazette*, a small local press that serviced all six dozen blocks of the hamlet, a community so minute mail delivery was only at the Post Office. Though Yaupon City was small it was important because it was at critical transportation crossroads. The largest industry in town wasn't really a business. It was a warehouse. Cargo coming from ships along the seaboard was transported to the warehouse where it was parceled out to trucks moving inland. Cargo from across the country that had to be shipped by sea from North Carolina ports was bulked to Yaupon City where it was separated out by seaport and then trucked to that port. The warehouse was the largest employer in Yaupon City and the rest of the businesses in the city were support.

While the city was small, it was large enough – and rich enough – to attract traveling shows. These shows were not as large as circuses but the city was on the Chautauqua circuit, one-man magician shows, small concerts, an occasional hypnotist, singers on tour for one-night stands and it did have a repertory theater building. Noonan had been through Yaupon City quite a few times and, like most residents of Sandersonville, was aware of the slur "Kinnakeeters, Yaupon Eaters!" He was also well aware of the consequences of drinking Yaupon tea; there was a very good reason its Latin name was *Ilex vomitoria*. Yaupon tea, like alcohol, is fine in small doses. VERY small doses.

Rolling forward to April 9th he started reading the paper. The high school production of Hamlet was in its third and final week There was a magician with a trained chimpanzee in town, a trio of mimes and a Civil War historian discussing the Battle of Gettysburg with a 3D presentation that using both modern and historic photographs. There were the usual deaths, births, social events and a couple of references to local award ceremonies and the weather reports.

Next Noonan placed a call to the Yaupon City Police Department, a force of three, one of them being the office manager. She was a pleasant woman and the first thing she said when Noonan said he was from Sandersonville was "Yaupon is a fine tea no matter what they say in Kinnakeet."

"I know," Noonan replied. "I have had Yaupon tea. Just not a lot of it."

The woman laughed. "I'm Shirley Hargreaves. What can I do for you, Captain?"

"I'm not sure. Just some fishing."

"Fishing better in Sandersonville than here – particularly if you are after ocean fish."

"No Red Drum today. I'm calling to see if anything in particular happened in mid-April in Yaupon City. You know, thefts, burglaries, robberies. Anything out of the ordinary."

"Nothing out of the ordinary happens in Yaupon City. Last April, eh? Let me think. We haven't had a robbery in about a year and most of the burglaries are related to drugs and we catch the perps fairly quickly. We have the usual: parking tickets, drunk drivers, drunk jay walkers, some petty theft. The only unusual thing that happened was a magician's chimpanzee got loose for a night. He wasn't gone long, let me tell you. The officers found him in a yaupon grove the next day and that chimp was sick, sick, sick. Other than that, nothing important.

"Do you have a pet store in town?"

"Two, actually."

"Do they sell fish?"

"Sure."

"How about fish tanks, aquariums."

"Salt and fresh water. Everything from goldfish to Arowana. I'm a fish person. My husband likes dogs."

"The pet stores sell dog food?"

"They sell everything. Yaupon City may be small but we are sophisticated."

Later that night Noonan – wearing a tie!!! – came for dinner at the Pamlico Lobster Pit with his wife Lorelei. Both took Lone by surprise: first, that Noonan was wearing a tie and, second, he was with his wife. Lorelei, an Alaskan who believed the only venerable crustacean was a King Crab caught in Alaskan waters, was leery of any creature from warm salt water.

"A surprise I must say," Lone said to Noonan.

"Yes, I know." He said. "Lorelei made me wear it."

"No, a surprise to see you more than once in a month. *And* with your wife."

"Well, duty calls. I have some more question for you but when I mentioned the Lobster Pit, well, here we are."

"And here you should be! I'll be along in a while. When there's a lull, we can talk."

Lorelei ordered crab cakes – commenting that she knew they would not be King Crab cakes – and Noonan ordered lobster – but not Louie. When they were through with their dinner, Lone came over for a chat.

"Did you find who got into my aquarium?"

"No one did. But I think I discovered how the ring got there."

"Do tell."

Noonan handed her a photocopy of an advertisement for Frank Blankenship, Magician *extraordinaire* and his trained chimp Speckles. Lone read the advertisement and then looked at Noonan questioningly.

"Last April Blankenship was in Yaupon City. He had a three-day run and the night of Day Two, Speckles made a break for freedom. He was gone most of the night and the next morning the police found him in a Yaupon grove."

"In a yaupon grove? I'll bet that was one sick monkey."

"You are correct."

"What does this have to do with the ring in Louie's tank?"

"Here's what I think happened. I don't know for a fact but I'll bet part of the magician's act involves a ring, the ring you found in Louie's aquarium. The chimp saw his chance for freedom and he beat feet into the Yaupon City warehouse. He probably got into a number of duck strip and chicken strip packages because they were found opened a few days later and the contents had to be given to the ASPCA. He also rustled through the aquarium supplies because they were found disturbed. I'm betting Speckles had a ring the magician uses in his act and dropped it in the aquarium supplies. While the warehouse could not sell the open duck and chicken strip bags, it could scoop up the aquarium supplies that were not damaged . . ."

". . . like the rocks," Lone said. "So the ring wasn't dropped in from the top of Louie's aquarium! It came in with the stones I used in the bottom of the salt water tank."

"That's what I think too."

"I'll bet that magician *extraordinaire* has been looking high and low for that ring!"

"I think that too."

"I think I'll give him a call. I'll tell him I've got a magic trick he can't match!"

THE MATTER OF THE REAPPEARING COELACANTH

Captain Heinz Noonan, the "Bearded Holmes" of the Sandersonville Police Department, was in a heated conversation with himself about the facts of life and how he was going to explain them to his twins when he was pulled back to reality when a large, stinking, molding fish was plopped on his desk by none other than the scourge of mankind, Commissioner Lizzard.

"What do you make of this?" Lizzard was ecstatic. "It's a coelacanth!"

"OK," said an unimpressed Noonan. "Are you going to eat it or stuff it?"

"Neither. I am going to donate it to a museum."

"A fish?"

"This is not just a *fish*. It's a coelacanth."

"It looks and smells like a fish to me," said Noonan smartly and then changed his tune when he saw Harriet over Lizzard's shoulder. She was shaking her head and wiggling a finger. "And you are showing me this fish because . . ." he let the sentence hang.

"First, it's not a *fish*, it's a coelacanth. You eat fish. This is a museum specimen."

"Because. . . ." Noonan let this sentence hang as well.

"A coelacanth is an extinct animal. It was supposed to have gone extinct with the dinosaurs."

"But here it is," said Noonan. "Not quite alive but it looks like it was alive so it could not be extinct."

"Exactly!" Lizzard became quite animated. "It was pulled from Pamlico Sound three days ago. A coelacanth! In Pamlico Sound! Three days ago!"

"And this is a police matter because . . ." Noonan was getting good at hanging sentences today.

"Because it is unclaimed property. No one is claiming it. So I am taking it to the Unclaimed Property Division. This is quite a coup, you know, having taking possession of the extinct fish."

"But it's not extinct if you are holding it and it was living three days ago. The dinosaurs died out a lot longer ago than that."

Lizzard was not listening. He had turned toward Harriet and Lt. Weasel who wiped smiles off their faces faster than a *Tyrannosaurus* would swallow a *titanosaur.* "Aren't you excited for Mother Nature?" he asked them. The two echoed something that have been and clearly was interpreted as "yes," "of course," "why not" and/or "most certainly." Turning back to Noonan, Lizzard said, "We need to get a chain of ownership of this coelacanth." He paused and then said, "for the records for unclaimed property."

"So," said Noonan finally catching the drift, "you want me to drive down the coast of Pamlico Sound looking for someone who lost an extinct fish that was abandoned three days ago?"

"Excellent," Lizzard explained. "You are a wonder, Captain. You read my mind completely. You can start at Butterfield Deep Sea Excursions. They are the ones who reported finding the coelacanth."

"They found it. Don't you mean they caught it?"

"No. They said they found it. Better yet, why don't you go ask them?" Noonan made a helpless gesture with his hands and indicated his desk covered with paperwork. Lizzard was impressed. "Go! Do your duty in the name of science!"

Lt. Weasel was quick to chime in. "This appears to be a two-man operation, Commissioner. I'll go with the Captain."

"Excellent!" said Lizzard turning toward Noonan. "We have an investigative team!"

"But it will need back-up," said Harriet quickly. "So I am volunteering my services!"

"Even better," chortled Lizzard. "Now we have secretarial skills onboard as well!"

Lizzard was facing Noonan so he could not see the daggers blasting out of Harriet's eyes.

It was an unbelievably horrible day to be away from the office. The temperature was in the mid-80s, there was not a cloud in the sky and every vehicle which contained a tourist was sequestered north of Virginia Beach. The roads were cluttered with sunshine and silence. Weasel made sure to collect both by driving the Sandersonville's sole convertible with its top down. Weasel kept the car traveling at a steady 45 miles per hour and when Noonan suggested he speed up, Harriet, sitting in the passenger seat with sunglasses and her right hand full of a cold, canned daiquiri, remarked that "speed kills." Noonan agreed so Weasel continued to drive a safe and sane 45 miles an hour all the way to Butterfield Deep Sea Excursions.

And then the fun began.

While there had not been many cars on the road to Butterfield Deep Sea Excursions, the parking lot at Butterfield Deep Sea Excursions was up to its gills in press vehicles. Noonan, Weasel and Harriet elbowed their way to the front of the mob. There was a guard at front holding back the press. Only after Noonan flashed his badge did the guard reluctantly let the three of them pass. Members of the press made unbroadcastable on-air comments as the trio made their way into the office of Butterfield Deep Sea Excursions.

Butterfield, the old man himself, was beside himself with a mixture of glee and regret. "I'm happy the press is here," he told Noonan after the captain had introduced himself, "because I can use the free publicity. But none of the press is going out and they are keeping customers from coming in."

"We'd be happy to go out," Harriet said quickly. "After all, this is police business and you can bill the Sandersonville Police Department for your assistance."

Noonan was about to say something but did not. Weasel did. "We are investigating a matter for the Department of Homeland Security. If you doubt us, feel free to contact Commissioner Lizzard at the Sandersonville Police Department."

"I'll take you at your word," Butterfield said to Harriet. "Does he go too?" He said pointing at Noonan.

"Absolutely," said Harriet. "He's part of our investigating team."

Butterfield rose to get one of his boats ready. When he left the room Noonan said to Harriet. "***Part*** of our investigating team. That was rich."

"So's he," snapped Harriet. "He isn't wearing a wedding ring. I'm not wearing a wedding ring. You and Weasel are going to be doing the investigating and I'll do the interrogating."

"A man with a boat," said Weasel slyly. "What more could you ask for on the Outer Banks?"

"A friend who has cabin on the shore of Pamlico Sound," Harriet retorted. "Which you have. And remember, I'm the one who got us out of the office today."

"I don't know what you've been told," John Butterfield told Noonan and Weasel. "My father and I run a small operation and this fish thing has gotten out of hand." Butterfield pointed at his father talking to Harriet at the stern of the craft. "We take parties out after local fish, Red Drum, Wahoo. When that, that . . ."

"Coelacanth," added Weasel.

"Yeah, that thing," said Butterfield. "It was a fish we had never seen before."

"A lot of people haven't," said Noonan. "Did you pull it off a hook?"

"No. It was already on board when I saw it. That's why I doubt we caught it. Our customers are city folk, the kind who don't like baiting hooks. So I don't think it was caught in the water. I think it was brought onto the boat."

"Why would someone do that?" Weasel thought like a cop. "Catching a fish like that would generate a lot of publicity for your business."

"You'd think so," the young man replied. "But it has been just the opposite. Sure, it's brought out the press but no one else. Everyone knows that, that,"

"Coelacanth," Weasel added.

"Yeah, whatever. We haven't seen an uptick of reservations. Everyone knows it's a phony. We look bad even though we haven't done anything wrong."

"Who actually caught the fish?" Noonan asked.

"A fine question, Captain. It's Captain isn't it?"

"Yes."

"A fine question. There were three people in the party. Out of New York. At least they said they were out of New York. They paid cash so we don't have a credit card receipt. They came aboard and fished all day. Just as we were about to return, they caught the fish."

"Or said they caught the fish."

"Yes."

"How far out were you?"

"Miles. We were nowhere near shore."

"How deep was the water there?"

"Very."

"That's quite an answer."

"Captain, we know where the fishing grounds are and get there with GPS. Our job is to keep the boat steady while our clients fish. I'm sure I knew how deep it was once but over the years I have forgotten that tidbit. My father and I use GPS to get here and GPS to get back. As long as the clients catch fish, we're happy. They're happy and tell their friends about us. It was great until that . . ."

"Coelacanth" Weasel cut in again.

". . .turned up."

"Why didn't they take the fish with them when they left?" Noonan asked.

"Good question. My answer: they didn't. They took their gear into the parking lot, loaded up a car and left. Poof. Gone. Never came back for the fish."

"What do you usually do with fish leftover on a trip?" Noonan was interested.

"Most of the time we give them to charity. Legally I suppose we could take them home and eat them but we don't want anyone ever saying we were overfishing for our own benefit."

"So it's not unusual for fish to be left onboard?"

"It's rare. We usually clean the fish and clients take the fillets home. Very few clients leave fish onboard."

"How did you know it was a coelacanth?"

"We didn't. It was a strange fish so we showed it to a Park Ranger. He said it was an extinct fish and called the cops. That's you guys, right?"

"Well," Weasel squirmed, "we are cops, yes. But we did not get the call. Someone else did. That's why the press showed up."

"You guys didn't call the press?"

"We don't do things like that," said Noonan. "What was the name of the Park Ranger you spoke with?

"I don't know. The guy who was there at the time. He took the fish and that was the last we saw of it."

Noonan was silent for a moment. Then he looked over the side of the boat and turned around. "How many clients can you take at a time?"

"Up to nine but we rarely have that many. Usually six."

"All in the same group?"

"Maybe. Sometimes we have three individuals and two groups of three. Or six individuals. Depends."

"These three people from New York. Did they rent the whole boat?"

"Yeah. And then said the others had backed out. They paid for the whole boat anyway.""In cash?"

"In cash."

Noonan scratched his head. "How's business been this year?"

"Good. It has not been a bad year. So if you are thinking that the, the,"

"Coelacanth" Weasel cut in again.

"Right. If you think the fish was a publicity stunt, you're wrong. We've got all the business we can handle. So has everyone else up and down the coast. Publicity is nice but we don't want clients who go out expecting to catch an extinct fish. And" he stopped for a moment and coughed, "I thought something that was extinct had been long dead. How can you catch something that's been dead for millions of years alive?"

"That," said Weasel, "is a very good question.

Harriet stayed on the boat "investigating" while Noonan and Weasel headed for the National Park. It was still a terrible day to be away from the office and the two men had committed an unforgiveable sin by forgetting to turn their cell phones on. Weasel claimed his cell phone battery was low; Noonan just stated his electronic beast was "sleeping and it is best to let sleeping dogs lie."

The story at the National Park was as bureaucratic as a sunrise. The Ranger in charge knew what he was looking at and turned "the specimen" which Noonan and Weasel called "a fish" over to the National Park biologist. The biologist put the fish in cold storage and called Homeland Security.

"Why," asked Weasel before Noonan could ask the same question, "would you call Homeland Security?"

The biologist rolled his eyes and pointed to a **BE PREPARED!** Homeland Security poster on the wall. "Because that's what my instructions are. See, here, Number 12. If anything out of ordinary happens I have to call Homeland Security in Washington D. C."

"So you called D. C."

"And what happened?"

"A guy named Lizard showed up."

"Lizzard?" Noonan said accenting the second "z."

"Probably the same guy. I told him what it was and he took off with it. I haven't seen it since."

"Do you see a lot of coelacanth around here?" asked Weasel with a straight face.

"Officer," said the biologist clearly looking for a name tag, "we never see coelacanth around here. Off the coast of Madagascar, yes, but that's a long way from here. Now, this one's an import. Why I cannot tell you."

"Let's try this from another angle," Noonan said. "Why would someone say they caught a coelacanth in these waters?"

"I have no idea," said the biologist. "If you know what a coelacanth is you know this fish was a plant. If you don't know what a coelacanth is you would probably care less. These are fishing waters, not scientific research waters." He took a breath. "And if you think it was done as a publicity stunt by some of the fishing boats, forget it. It's a good year. They don't need any publicity."

"So you're stuck for an answer?"

"Call Lizzard. He said he had a crackerjack detective in Sandersonville. Why not ask him?"

Weasel did not crack a smile.

Noonan and Weasel struggled to make it back to Sandersonville by close of business – and failed. Weasel dropped Noonan off at the station to retrieve his car and, as it was Friday, Weasel decided to keep the city car for the weekend because he did not want to check the car in after office hours and run up overtime on the garage staff. It was going to be another terrible, Saturday, and Sunday was not going to be any better so Weasel swore he would take good care of the car before he turned it in on Monday. Harriet had declined a ride back to the office and stated she would "do just fine" so they left her at Butterfield Deep Sea Excursions.

As it turned out, both Saturday and Sunday were miserable days for Noonan. In addition to weed plucking, dirt moving, gravel spreading and dog poop picking upping he suffered the indignity of chauffeuring the twins to a skating party and a movie while his wife waited at home with spade and bucket in hand. Then she complained as to how hard supervising was.

It was not until Sunday night that Noonan was able to turn on the internet and do research on coelacanth. He learned absolutely nothing he did not know. But he did pick up a new term, "passive drift feeders" which meant the fish just went where the current took it and ate what came floating by, the antediluvian equivalent of "going with the flow." Its meat was not tasty and its oil unusable. The only people who wanted the species were fish biologists.

So why fake the catching of a Madagascar fish off the coast of North Carolina?

That was such a good question Noonan did not have answer.

Noonan was not caught by surprise when Commissioner Lizzard came into his office at the crack of dawn – 10 a. m. for Lizzard because that was the crack of his dawn – and demanded to know why Noonan's cell phone had been turned off all weekend. A fake-surprised Noonan reached for his phone and saw its power was extinct. He showed the phone to Lizzard who pointed to the power cord on Noonan's desk.

"You missed my calls," he snapped.

"If I had known you were calling I'd have answered," Noonan replied with a hundred mile stare.

"Well?" Lizzard asked.

"Well, what?"

"The coelacanth."

"Ah, yes, the coelacanth. You picked it up from the biologist at the National Park."

"Correct."

"And it is downstairs in unclaimed property."

"Negative. It is on its way to Washington D. C. There ***is a lot of*** interest in that fish."

"Why? It's obviously a fake."

"Who knows? It could be part of a plot."

"Really? What kind of a plot?"

"Well, not really a *plot* as in plot-plot. But there has been ***a lot of talk*** about global warming and this coelacanth could be proof."

"That the oceans are warming up? We don't need proof. It's happening."

"The coelacanth is more proof positive. An African fish showing up off the coast of North Carolina. A fish from a hot continent showing on a hot coast."

"Commissioner, that fish was a plant. Someone wanted to generate publicity for . . ." and the scales fell from his eyes.

"Hardly," continued Lizzard. "Why I hear a salt-water crocodiles turned up down the coast from Marvin City. They are usually only found in hot climates like Egypt. Why would they show up here?"

"Marvin City," mused Noonan. "That's not in our county."

"Who knows? The water is warm enough the salt water crocodiles could be headed this way."

"Really? Let me guess, Homeland Security has a watch out for salt water crocodiles."

"Anything suspicious, out of the ordinary. When it turns up, we investigate."

"Who's the *we* that's going to be investigating these *out of the ordinary* circumstances?"

"Now that the coelacanth has turned up in this county and the salt water crocodiles further south, I am going to be requesting more money from Homeland Security for the two adjoining counties."

"But my report. . ." Noonan did not get a chance to finish.

"Oh, you don't have to produce a report, Captain. I've already done it. We discovered a strange species of fish in our waters which we sent on to Washington D. C."

"You didn't put my name on the report did you?"

"Oh no," Lizzard said as he gave a look of horror. "This is way above your pay grade."

Noonan was relieved. "Let me guess, Homeland Security was handed a dead salt water crocodile which was found down the coast below Marvin City."

"It did. How'd you guess?"

"I'm psychic.

THE MATTER OF THE REVERSE DINNER BELL

Captain Heinz Noonan, the "Bearded Holmes" of the Sandersonville Police Department, was in the process of doing his annual office personnel performance reports and was stumped when he came upon that of Lt. George Weasel. He was stumped not because Weasel's performance had been below standard – which it had not been – but because the man's name had changed since the previous year. There was a new label over the name and it read "Billy-Bob George Handsome Weasel."

"Handsome?" Noonan said softly.

"Right!" yelled Harriet from across her desk across the room. "You'll love the story."

"How do you know what I am looking at?" Noonan snapped as he looked up.

"P-l-e-a-s-e! You said *Handsome*. We all," she pointed around the room to a half-dozen smiling faces, "know what you are reading. Handsome George. Who knew?"

"Why'd he change his name?"

"Why not ask him," Harriet said and pointed to Billy-Bob George Handsome Weasel as he lumbered like a hippopotamus toward Noonan's desk.

Noonan held up the file as if to say "And?" as Billy-Bob George Handsome Weasel sat down.

"It's a short story," he said.

"I've got time for a novel," snapped Noonan and handed him the file.

"My uncle, Handsome Weasel, left me a small cabin on Pamlico Sound. I had to claim it by using my full legal name. The minute that happened I had to change all names on all documents to Billy-Bob George Handsome Weasel. See," he said as he pulled out his wallet and showed Noonan his new driver's license, "I'm officially and legally Billy-Bob George Handsome Weasel on all my documents." He tapped his Annual Performance file. "Including that one."

"How efficient of you," said Noonan with half a grin. "What do we call you around here?"

"How about lt." He was stone-faced. "Until I make captain and then you-all can call me captain."

"Or corporal if you backslide."

"If I back slide it will be to a cabin on the shore of Pamlico Sound." He paused for a moment and then said, "Now that I'm here I'd like to discuss a difficulty that came up."

"Does it involve getting rid of a handsome ghost in your cabin on the shore of Pamlico Sound?" Noonan chuckled at his own pun.

"Partially. It involves crocodiles, ship bells and Russian rats."

"Now let me see if I've got this straight," Noonan was still shaking his head. "From the story that told me, you've got marauding salt water crocodiles from the waters of Pamlico Sound which are coming ashore on your uncle's, that is, your property to scavenge Russian rats and your uncle has been trying to scare them away with ship's bells on trip wires."

"That's the size of it, sir."

"Call me Heinz."

"Yes, sir."

"That went well."

"What, sir?"

"Never mind. I do not want this to come as a shock to you but your story has a lot of holes, so to speak."

"Really?"

"First, the only crocodiles in the United States are in zoos. Second, even if there were salt water crocodiles, they would not chase Russian rats. The rats are too fast. Crocodiles wallow in the shallows like logs and surprise animals that come to the shoreline to drink. Third, even if crocodiles did forage for Russian rats, I don't see that a trip wire would be any good. If a crocodile hit a trip wire all the bell would do was ring. I don't see that scaring crocodiles off – if there were crocodiles to scare off."

"That's all?"

"You want more? I think those fantasies are a good start."

Weasel had a comeback. "First, there are salt water crocodiles in the United States that are not in zoos. They started in the waters off Florida where they were released as pets. As there was nothing to eat them, they grew large and then started moving up the coast. Now those crocs have not made it this far north," he paused for emphasis, "yet," and gave another pause, "but the salt water crocodiles on Pamlico Sound are from a crocodile farm that was established during the Second World War. The military was studying the animals as part of war effort. After the war they closed down the farm."

"Let me guess," postulated Noonan. "Some of the crocodiles wandered off into the yaupon bushes and were never seen again."

"Not *never again*," said Weasel. "Just not often. There are still some out there. And they occasionally feed."

"On your uncle's property."

"Yes. On Russian rats."

"Do the bells scare the crocodiles away?"

"No. The bells are to scare the Russian rats away. When they go, the crocodiles go."

"Kind of a reverse dinner bell."

"I guess you could say that, Captain."

"I just did. Now, is there a reason you are telling me this tall tale?"

"It's not a tall tale, sir. It's the root a very old mystery on Tabor Island."

"I've never heard of Tabor Island."

"Most people have not. It's a mythical island."

Noonan looked across his desk over his glasses at Lt. Weasel and then at Harriett who was rolling her eyes. Then he looked back at Weasel.

"OK. So the footloose salt water crocodiles who do not eat Russian rats because they are being scared away by trip wires on ship bells are part of a tall tale of an imaginary island. Do I have that right?"

"Yes, sir."

"This story has progressed so well I'm sure there are more moving parts."

"Moving parts?"

"More unusual aspects of the story."

"You mean like the phantom seagulls?"

"I would never have guessed."

"They are not phantom as in *phantoms,* you know. They are just all grey and appear ghostly. That's why they are called phantom gulls."

"And they fit into the story of the salt water crocodiles who escaped from a World War II experimental facility," Noonan stalled and Weasel finished.

". . . who forage for the Russian rats who are scared away by ships' bells attached to tripwire. Yes, sir."

Noonan was silent for a moment. "Well," he said finally. "Your uncle, the one who left you his property. He must have been very concerned about living there. I mean, with those sea crocodiles wandering all over the landscape. He didn't get eaten did he?"

"Oh, no. He was very careful. He spent a lot of time on the property putting up fences and the like. You know, to keep the crocodiles off the property."

"Are you going to be spending a lot of time on the property?"

"Well, yes. Of course. I'm going to be selling my home here in town and moving out there. It will be my retirement home-in-progress, so to speak. It will take longer to get to work but the drive will be worth it. I guess I'll be coming to work a bit later than normal because of the drive, you know."

Noonan thought for a moment. "Did I ever tell you about the monkey and the crocodile?"

"Sorry?"

"The monkey and the crocodile. It's a one of those moral stories. Once upon a time there was a monkey who lived in an apple tree. One day a crocodile – a hungry crocodile – came swimming by and the monkey gave the crocodile an apple."

"Really?" said Weasel. "Crocodiles don't eat apples."

"In this story they do," Noonan replied.

"Yes, sir."

"Well, the crocodile ate the apple and found it delicious. So the monkey gave him another one and another one. See, the monkey could give the crocodile apples because the monkey was in the tree where the apples were."

"Is this going somewhere?"

"Absolutely. The more apples the crocodile ate the more he liked the monkey. So they became great friends."

"As long as the monkey kept feeding the crocodile apples."

"That's correct. Now this friendship upset the crocodile's wife to no end so she demanded that her husband trick the monkey into taking a ride on her husband's back and then, when the monkey was least expecting it, the crocodile was to devour the monkey and bring her the monkey's heart."

"Heart?"

"Heart, yes. The crocodile didn't want to kill his friend but, you know, his wife and all."

"I'm not married."

"Yet."

"Go on."

"So the crocodile lured the monkey onto his back. He said he'd take the monkey around the lagoon and when the two were far out in the water the crocodile confessed to the monkey he needed the monkey's heart to keep his wife happy."

"That must have distressed the monkey to no end," said Weasel.

"True. But the monkey was no fool. He told the crocodile that he didn't have his heart with him. It was back in the tree. If the crocodile really wanted a monkey heart, he'd be glad to give it to him."

"But the hearts was back in the tree, right?"

"Correct."

"Let me guess, the crocodile was stupid enough to take the monkey back to the tree and once there, the monkey made it back up into the branches and said 'Sorry, Charlie.'"

"Correct again. The moral of the story being that the world is full of fools."

"Sounds like a crock to me," said Weasel and chuckled at his play on words.

"Could be," said Noonan. "It's like your story of trip wires on ships bells to scare away Russian rats to keep sea crocodiles off the property which is associated with a mythical island with phantom gulls where you will be living so you have to come in late every day. It has a lot in common with the story of the monkey and the crocodile."

"Really? What?"

"Well, both are tales."

THE MATTER OF THE EVANESCING ELIXIR

Captain Noonan, the "Bearded Holmes" of the Sandersonville Police Department, was seated beside the Sandersonville City Pool when he knew he was about to be accosted. It did not take the eyes of a seasoned detective to realize the accosting was about to take place. It only took open eyes. The man doing the accosting was of average height, average weight, had eyes of an indistinguishable color and brown hair which could be seen at a distance. As the man drew closer, the eyes were perceivable as blue. What gave away the accosting was the fact that the man in question was dressed as a police officer while the rest of the Sandersonville City Pool rabble were dressed for the weather, swelter and swimming pool.

"Let me guess," snapped the "Bearded Holmes" without adjusting his sun glasses on his temple. "You have come with a problem only I can solve."

"No," replied the man. "I've come with a problem I've already solved and thought you might want to hear the story."

"And why might I want to hear the story?"

"Because it is a case where the goods are gone but the gone goods are water under the bridge, so to speak. Besides, your secretary said you needed a laugh."

"OK, I'll buy that. What's the story about?"

"Water. Stolen. 8,000 gallons."

Noonan did not bat an eye. He had been on more than his fair share of law-and-order merry-go-rounds. That's what he told the stranger – who was an Alaska State Police detective – and then asked, "Let me get this right. Someone in Alaska stole 8,000 gallons of water and you came all the way to North Carolina, to a swimming pool, on the Outer Banks, dressed in your uniform, in the middle of the summer, the best time to be in Alaska, to tell me this?"

"Not exactly," the man replied. He stuck out his head, "Detective Stephan Gregory. I'm out of Petersburg and I know," he looked at Noonan sideways with a knowing smirk, "you know where Petersburg is."

"I know where Petersburg is," Noonan snapped back with a similar smirk, "but Petersburg is not large enough for a State Police station and probably only has three police officers at best."

"Yup, you got that right. No, I'm on assignment there, so to speak. My actual office is in Palmer but I was sent to Petersburg to solve a unique crime."

"A unique crime? In Petersburg? A city of, what, 3,000? On assignment? There's not a lot of crime in Petersburg. What does it have to do with 8,000 gallons of water and, again, why are you here on the Outer Banks."

"Answering the second question first: wahoo. My wife is big into wahoo. But she doesn't like Hawaii. So, when she discovered she could get wahoo along the Outer Banks, well, here we are."

"From Alaska?"

"From Alaska. As far as you can get from Palmer and still speak English."

"And why are you in uniform?"

"The law and order convention in Nags Head. That's what brought us here. Companion fare and convention, cheaper than two tickets to Hawaii. I was expecting to see you at the convention, captain. I was going to tell you my story there. When you weren't there, I came here. It was my excuse to see the Cape Hatteras lighthouse anyway. It's the tallest in the United States and moved 2,900 feet in 1999. I'd never heard of a lighthouse moving."

"We've got some strong winds here on the Outer Banks."

"Do tell," Gregory responded. "Now my question for you: Why weren't you at the law and order conference?"

Noonan snickered. "I'd never be a member of any organization that would have me as a member."

Gregory snickered back. "That's not original. It's from Groucho Marx."

"As true today as the when he spoke it. Now, the water?"

"Are you aware of what is being called the 'Alaska Cold Rush?'"

"Sure. It's the growing trend of collecting glacier ice and selling it as ice in a punch bowl or as the water in cosmetics and liquor. Glacier ice and glacier bergs are popular because the ice is a deep blue and is tens of thousands of years old. Created back in the days before all water on the planet was polluted with all kinds of nasty things. Is Petersburg part of the Alaska Cold Rush?"

"Absolutely. In the off-season, fishing boats harvest the floating glacier bergs. Those guys are called 'iceberg cowboys,' by the way. They haul the glacier bergs to the Petersburg dock where the vodka company hauls them into the distillery. The bergs are heated and converted into water and mixed with whatever makes vodka. Thus the water is transformed into Petersburg Glacier Vodka. It's pricy but the distillery employs a dozen people which helps the local economy."

"Let me guess," Noonan pointed at a raised eyebrow. "Someone stole the water from the distillery."

"Yes, but it's a good bet they thought they were stealing the vodka. Petersburg is a small town. Everyone knows everyone else's business so the thieves had to have come in barge to drain the tank. You can't hide that kind of tanker truck in Petersburg and there are no roads out of the city. The only way the water could have left town was in a barge. The water probably made it all the way to Juneau with no one the wiser."

"How could the thieves *not know* they were stealing water instead of vodka?"

"The whole distillery smells of vodka. There were only two large tanks, one for the glacier and the other for water. It's was probably an eeny, meeny, miny, moe and they ended up with the water, not the vodka. Best guess, they were going to rebottle the vodka and sell it cheap. Street value, so to speak, is about $20 a quart which makes the 8,000 gallons worth about $650,000. Not bad for one night's work."

"Could they sell the water."

"Unlikely. Glacier water is an expense, not an asset. It's labor intensive. They get it by corralling glaciers at sea, dragging them into Petersburg, cutting them in slabs which are then melted. It's the publicity that makes the water valuable. Glacier water does not taste any different than filtered water. It's the romance of the glacier," he accented the word *glacier,* "that makes it exotic."

"OK," Noonan said as he dropped his sunglasses from his brow to his nose, "is there a reason you are telling me this story?"

"No really. I was just in the neighborhood and you've got a reputation for the unusual."

"But why was the Alaska State Police investigating?"

"Insurance. Petersburg Glacier Vodka needed a police report to file a claim."

"Are you sure the water was stolen?"

"I know the vodka wasn't. There's no reason for Petersburg Glacier Vodka to fake stolen water. Even if they did, it's a loss to them. They can't use regular water as a substitute and it's going to cost them to get more glacier bergs. Product slowed so there is a dollar loss. No, I don't see any incentive for Petersburg Glacier Vodka to steal their own water."

"And there's no way for the water to have leaked out?"

"They could have opened a valve and drained the water tank in the Petersburg Bay but I don't see that happening. I mean, why? There's not a dime in doing that. As far as a leak is concerned, I did an extensive walkthrough and saw no evidence of a leak. Even if the leak had been intentional, they could have replaced the glacier water with distilled water. Both taste the same. No one would have been the wiser. Besides, everyone in Petersburg knew of the theft the morning after. It even made into the newspapers in Southeast Alaska. You can't keep a secret is a small town – or a bunch of them."

Noonan was silent for a moment. Then he finally said, "Let's suppose, let's just suppose there really was a thief. [Pause] But he was actually after the water, not the vodka."

Gregory guffawed, "Why?!"

"Well, suppose he had a rich client, say in Japan, who wanted glacier water ice cubes. All the thief would have to do was steal the glacier water and refreeze it. This time in small cubes."

"That would be a lot of effort and a lot of risk. Petersburg is a small town so the nearest place to refreeze the water would be Juneau, about100 miles away. There's a lot of miles where a boat with 8,000-gallon tank could be spotted."

"Oh, I don't think the water left Petersburg."

"What?"

"Here's what think happened. Someone in Petersburg cut a deal with someone who wanted a lot of glacier water, liquid or cubed I don't know. Either way, it makes no difference. What the person needed was the illusion of theft."

"What do you mean 'illusion of theft?'"

Noonan smiled. "There is no chemical or taste difference between glacier water and filtered water. They are both water. But the glacier water has the romance. It's exotic. So the thief sold his client on the romance of glacier water. Then he slipped into the distillery and drained the glacier water tank."

"But no tanker boat was in the area and all of the tanker trucks in Petersburg were accounted for."

"The thief didn't take the water. He didn't want the water. He wanted the headlines. He just drained the glacier water into Petersburg Bay. The newspaper said the glacier water had been stolen. That was his proof of the theft. Then he sold his client distilled water, or distilled water in cubes, as glacier water. Probably out of Juneau. You can fly that kind of cargo out of Juneau, not Petersburg. As long as the water came out of Southeast Alaska, the client would have to assume the water he bought was the stolen glacier water."

"So the water was just drained into the bay?"

"Probably. It had no value. The newspaper story had the value."

"And we got zip. We were played!"

"Don't beat yourself up, there's still an end game."

"I don't see how, the water's gone and the thief has cash in his pocket."

"We'll see."

A week later Harriet came into Noonan's office with a box.

It was empty.

Noonan looked inside the box and then at Harriet questioningly. "You bring me an empty box?"

"Well, it wasn't empty when it arrived. It had two bottles of vodka. Petersburg Glacier Vodka, as a matter of fact. I took them home."

"What?!"

"You can't take gifts or gratuities," she snapped. "I can. If you want the bottles back, I'll bring them in tomorrow."

"Empty?"

"No other way to return vodka bottles."

"Was anything else in the box?"

"A newspaper."

"Ah," said Noonan, the scales falling from his eyes. "I'll bet there was a story about the recovery of 8,000 gallons of glacier water."

Harriet tapped her forehead with her right index finger tip. "You are psychic. Let me guess, that Alaska State Policeman with the wild story."

"Yup. I convinced him to fight fire with fire. The glacier water was never stolen, it was just drained out of the tank. What thief wanted was the headlines in the local paper. Then he sold distilled water as glacier water. The buyer never knew the difference."

"So you had him gin up the alleged discovery of the 8,000 gallons . . ."

"Very good. You could be a detective. Right. Now the buyer of the supposedly stolen glacier water is going to have a heart-to-heart with the thief. Probably demand his money back. As Shakespeare said, he will have been hoisted on his own petard."

"How do you know the thief if a man?"

"I don't."

"If it had been a women she would have gotten away with it."

"How do you know that?"

"Women are smarter than me."

"Really?"

"Absolutely," Harriet said as she tapped the empty box on Noonan's desk. "Who got the glacier water vodka and who got left to sup up day-old coffee he had to buy with his own money?"

THE MATTER OF THE PURLOINING IN THE PENINSULA COUNTY LAND FILL

Captain Noonan, the "Bearded Holmes" of the Sandersonville Police Department, was having a pleasant lunch at his favorite restaurant in Anchorage. He was on vacation, his wife was his boys were with their grandfather. That gave him the entire afternoon to himself. His wife also had the rental car leaving him to take a taxi home, a blessing in disguise for it meant that he could have wine with his lunch, a rare treat in the world of law and order.

JENS' was the perfect place for such a diversion. It was the epitome of subtle charm; the reason Noonan visited the restaurant every time he came to Alaska. The cuisine and decor were European in the bistro-around-the-corner-style. Hard liquor was not served but the choice of wines was the most eclectic on the West Coast. Noonan was savoring his second glass of a New Zealand Merlot while Lorelei was either spending too much money at the Nordstrom or dawdling at David Green Master Furrier where she was undoubtedly stroking mink and contemplating how to make it out the front door with a muskrat coat less a shoplifting charge.

Jens, owner and *impresario* of the restaurant as well as the very soul of discretion, delicately tapped Noonan on the shoulder and whispered that there was a woman on the phone for him in his, Jens', office. Noonan popped open his pocket watch, shook his head sadly, and then followed Jens' back to the office. He picked up the phone cradle that was lying on the desk and started talking before his lips came within speaking distance of the mouthpiece.

"No, my Love, you may not have a fur. It's too expensive. Maybe after the boys are out of college."

"That's fine with me," a soft female voice cooed from the other end of the line, "I prefer silk myself. Fur is too hot for Florida and, frankly, I'd prefer to spend my time hunting for manatees with a camera than fishing for compliments at the Peninsula City Chamber of Commerce." Noonan stalled for a moment as he stared at the instrument in his hand. When he didn't say anything in response, the voice came again. "Captain Noonan, are you there?"

"Yes, I am. I thought I was talking to my wife."

"Well, if I see her I'll tell her that furs are too expensive and not socially functional, even if you live in Sandersonville."

"Thank you very much. And you are. . .?"

"I'm Detective Geraldine Blakely of the Peninsula City and County Sheriff's Office. I'm not going to tell you how I got your name because I'm catching you on vacation."

"Commissioner Lizzard has been loose with his lips again, right."

"I'm sworn to secrecy."

"All right, Detective Blakely. I'll bite. Why are you calling?"

"We've got a problem down here in Peninsula County that is unusual . . ."

"That's usually why I get called."

"Yes, sir. That's what I've been told. What makes this problem so pressing isn't so much what happened but who the perps were and what was found on their person."

"Surprise me."

"We had some reports of strange activities at the local land fill so we staked out the area . . ."

"Land fill, as in garbage dump."

"We prefer to call it a sanitary land fill but, yes, it's a garbage dump."

"You're kidding, right? You caught perps digging into a garbage dump?"

"Yes, sir, caught them actually. And no, sir, I'm not kidding. It was a simple stakeout. I mean, who would believe anyone would be stealing anything from a garbage dump?"

"You're right. I don't believe it."

"Well, we caught them all right. It turns out that three of the four perps were, as some of my co-workers say, *pretty bad dudes.* Two of them were wanted on federal weapons charges, for smuggling lots and lots of guns, illegal flight to avoid prosecution, armed robbery and kidnapping."

"What nice fellows."

"Actually they are women. A third was about to go to trial under RICO charges and was out on bail for two murders in New York which relate to the largest cocaine bust in that city's history."

"That must have been one heck of a cocaine bust!"

"It was. Something like three boxcars of the substance. It was being smuggled in as experimental chemical for livestock weight enhancement experiments."

"Cute. The third was a woman too?"

"How'd you guess?"

"Just smart. They're all women, right?"

"That's right."

"OK. I can't stand the suspense. Tell me about the fourth."

"This'll be a twist for you. The fourth is a *non sequitur*. Widowed mother of four. No priors. No aliases. Life-long resident of Peninsula County. Social pillar of the community. Net worth about five million, give or a take a few hundred thousand. Son at Harvard. Daughter at Bryn Mawr. Two others away in prep school."

"Hardly the kind to be with the other three. Was she there under duress?"

"No. She appeared to be calling the shots."

"OK. Now, what made it so important that you call me on vacation?"

"The fourth perp, the *non sequitur* had a timing device in her possession. But it was running in reverse. When we picked them up – about ten hours ago – the timer read 131 hours."

"And they won't tell you diddly, right?"

"Yeah. You got it. The two *real bad dudes* we put on ice. The other two we had to release."

"Not illegal to wander around on a sanitary land fill, eh?"

"Right. They didn't even bother to ask for a lawyer."

"Did they have any equipment with them?"

"Shovels, dosing rods, metal detector and an arthroscopic camera on a ten-foot cable."

"I doubt that any of that stuff is going to help them with whatever they were looking for."

"That's what we thought."

"Were they standing in one place or wandering."

"Oh, they were standing and digging in one place when they were apprehended. There is no evidence of other digging in the general area."

"Do you know where the garbage came from?"

"Yes and no. Yes, it came from the residents of Peninsula County during the month of May – as in three months ago. As far as which subdivision, nope, haven't a clue."

"Was anything else unusual found with the perps?"

"Unusual? What's *usual* about this group? Let's see. All of them had wallets: ain't that a laugh. We checked all the wallets. Nothing out of the ordinary. Credit cards, theirs, about $200 in cash, family pictures, spare house keys, yadda, yadda, yadda. Two of them had pocket knives, one had a pen and pad – with no writing on the pad, let me quickly add. Yes, I know, check the pad for impressions of writing. We did that last night and found zip. All of them had keys. All of them were wearing pants. All of them had belts. That's it."

"What kind of shoes were they wearing?"

"Shoes? That's an odd question. Let's see. Three of them were wearing what we call combat boots down here, you know, like hiking boots. The *non sequitur* was wearing Reeboks. New. As in brand new."

"Did you do an analysis of the shoe bottoms?"

"Sorry. No."

"Too late to get a search warrant?"

"For what?" Blakely laughed. "We are talking about Ms. Peninsula County here. There isn't a judge in Florida that will give me a search warrant when the charge is digging in a public garbage dump."

"I kind of thought that would be the case."

"Well, sir, now you know about all I know. Is there anything else I can do to help you?"

"You seem quite confident I can solve this oddity of the criminal world."

"Yes, sir. Our commissioner says you're the only one in America who can do it and your commissioner feels the same way."

"He would," Noonan replied helplessly, "I solve the problems and he gets the glory."

"Welcome to the wonderful world of law and order, captain."

"I'm not sure I can help you, detective. But I'll do what I can. Let's see. I'll give you the FAX at my brother-in-law's house but I'll need some more information. But, like I said, I don't know how much I can do for you. Take the exact moment – and I mean the exact moment – when the timer will expire and compare that with everything you can there in Peninsula County, court appearances, weather reports, high school graduations, tour ship arrivals and departures, flight arrivals and departures, military exercises, time locks on banks. Anything. Do the same thing for New York. Send me what you can on the other three perps. I don't think that will help much but see what you can find. Since our commissioners are pushing this so hard, have your commissioner call Commissioner Harold Wilkerson in New York."

"We've already started on that."

"Good. Second, try for a search warrant. Yeah, I know you may not get it but give it a shot. But only for our *non sequitur.* She's our key. If you get that search warrant, go for long distance calls too. Casually talk to the mailman, neighbors, lawn care people, pool maintenance, whoever. If they knew where they were digging they must have talked to someone at the solid waste facility. Take a look at her bank account, investment portfolio. See what you can dig up about her past. Does she have a college degree? In what? What did her husband do? Where did the money come from? How did the husband die? When did he die? Any court cases involving her husband?"

"Most of that stuff we already have and it's useless. Our non sequiter was involved in another case."

"Another case? Involving this woman?"

"Yes. There was a law suit."

"This is rich. Dare I ask what the law suit was about?"

"A vagrant cat. It is alleged . . ."

"How alleged is this alleged?"

"I'd say it was true but the police don't get involved in civil matters."

"OK. What is alleged that was probably true?"

"That a cat was pooping in a neighbor's yard."

"That's the law suit?"

"Yup."

"Don't the people in Peninsula County have anything better to do than sue each other over cat poop?"

"I didn't file the suit. Apparently there was another allegation . . ."

"Oh joy. How alleged was this one?"

"Garbage, if you ask me. It was alleged that the cat poop was damaging the surface feeding ability of some prize Camellia flowers."

"What were the damages?"

"Filed or awarded?"

"I'll bite, both."

"Mrs. Hendershoting sued for $500,000 in damages and $500,000 in pain and suffering."

"Pain and suffering? That's novel. Her's or the Camellia's?"

"Who knows? She lost the case because she could not prove that the poop she extracted from her garden was indeed that of the cat in question or some other, and I quote, 'peripatetic feline.'"

"Talk to Mrs. Hendershoting. She probably doesn't have a nice thing to say about our perp."

"Mrs. Hendershoting *is* our perp. The other party was an out-of-state corporation."

"How can an out-of-state corporation own a cat in Florida?"

"Exactly what the judge asked."

"And our perp said?"

"She said the poop belonged to the cat and the cat belonged to the corporation so the corporation was illegal polluting her yard. She also filed complaints with the Florida departments of clean water, sanitation, regulatory commission as well as the EPA and ASPCA."

"This is the woman worth $5 million that's been digging in the garbage dump?"

"I never said this was an easy case."

"OK. Let me think on it. Get me that information as soon as you can."

"Yes, sir."

"And call me, Heinz."

As soon as Blakely hung up, Noonan placed a call to the Peninsula City and County Sheriff's Office in Florida. He asked for Geraldine Blakely and got her voice mail. The voice matched so Noonan was willing to believe that the call had been legitimate. Being in Alaska, one could never be too sure. After all, this was the land of absurding where it was a state sport to hoodwink gullible Outsiders on the most outlandish stories imaginable.

The first thing Noonan did after lunch – besides begging his wife over the cell phone to forget about buying a fur coat – was to take a cab out the Anchorage land fill. He had no trouble at all talking with the manager and the cabbie was more than pleased to sit and read the newspaper while the meter ran.

"You're with the Sandersonville Police and you want to talk about an Alaskan landfill?"

"Well, that's not exactly what I meant. I just have a few questions?"

"You're the first cop that ever wanted to talk about a garbage problem."

"Not a lot of crime happening out here?"

"Hey, you can have whatever you find out here."

"I imagine that's the case everywhere in the country?"

"Probably. Our problem is what people are bringing in; not what they're taking out."

"Like what?"

"Oh, you want to get technical? You can dump anything except toxic and hazardous items like paint, dynamite, tar, refrigerators, oil, batteries, chemicals and dead bodies."

"You get a lot of dead bodies?"

"Got one last winter. A drunk died in a dumpster and we didn't know about it until his cadaver fell out of the truck. No, we don't get a lot of 'em. The three we've had since I've been manager have all been DOA, if that's the correct term to use in a land fill. There was no crime associated with them."

"How long have you been the manager here?"

"Eight years."

"Can you tell where your garbage came from in the land fill?"

"If you mean can I walk to the exact spot where the Muldoon Route 7 garbage from last year is buried, not exactly. I can come close. Last week I can be a bit more specific. But it's not that easy. Garbage is not something that is compartmentalized. Each day one-sixth of the city has its garbage collected. It's dumped into the land fill in the order the trucks make it here. Then it's mixed with garbage that comes in daily from people driving in and dropping household garage. Everything is crushed with rollers – those at the big bulldozer-like pieces of equipment you can see rolling around on the landfill. When they aren't pulverizing garbage they are rolling down earth. Every three or four feet of garbage is covered with a layer of dirt. That's how the landfill is built."

"If I wanted to find something that had been collected three months ago, how close could I get?"

"If and if and if and if I'd say somewhere in a circle about 30 feet across to a depth of four or five feet. But that is a lot of garbage, something like 300 cubic yards. Unless it was really big, I don't think you would find it – unless you had the 101st Airborne helping you."

"Is there anything that would help me find an object?"

"How big?"

"I don't know."

"I can't think of anything. A metal detector wouldn't help because there is so much metal."

"How about dosing wires?"

"Dosing wires? Aren't they used for finding water?"

Noonan shrugged his shoulders. "Is there anything I could use to find something that was four feet down?"

"About the only thing I can think of would be some kind of a camera on a cable. They use those kinds of things to look for living people in collapsed buildings. But people are pretty big things, if you know what I mean. Since you don't know what you are looking for, I don't know what to tell you."

"Well, thanks for your time."

"Was this a joke, by the way? I mean, who tries to dig up something that's already been dumped? Usually when something is dumped, it's gone forever."

Noonan's next stop was an arthroscopic surgeon who laughed at more questions than he answered. Then Noonan visited a fire station where he talked about equipment used to find trapped people in a collapsed building and was told that you had to know the people where there before you went looking for them. Once it was established that people had been in the building, the best initial piece of equipment was a dog. The razzle-dazzle probes worked adequately in a collapsed building because they could be snaked into and out tight spots in the general vicinity of where the dogs indicated the people would be. A landfill was different because everything was compacted so there was no room to run the cable.

Everyone thought dousing rods were for water.

When he returned to his brother-in-law's home, the FAXes waiting for him offered no clues. He was still pondering the situation when he got his second call from Blakely.

"Did your wife buy the fur coat?"

"Shhhhhhh! Don't even whisper the word."

"Sorry," Blakely said in a hush. Then, in a normal voice, "There's been a development."

"Let me guess," said Noonan thoughtfully. "The federal government has stepped in and seized jurisdiction."

"How, how did you know that?"

"Just a guess. From the documents that you FAXed I see all the women are in their upper 60s, early 70s. These aren't perps. They're matrons."

"We got the list of their crimes off NCIC. That's all we've got."

"Their last names are interesting. All Anglo in an area where Latinos outnumber the Anglos. Let me also guess that they are all Cuban and their Anglo names are those of their husbands."

"That's also a good guess – and accurate. How did you know that?"

"Lucky guess. Did you find out who our prime suspect's husband was?"

"He was Anglo and worked for a multi-national import-export firm. He specialized in selling agricultural farm equipment, tractors and combines. That kind of thing. Primarily to South American countries and large corporations."

"So he flew out of the country a lot?"

"I would presume so. It would be my guess that the largest buyer of agricultural equipment in the Western Hemisphere would be South American farmers. The Miami area would be the best place to live."

"Good point. Do you still have the file on that cat poop case?"

"Yyyyesss, why?"

"I'd like some information."

"I can get it on line. What did you need to know?"

"What was the name of the out-of-state company she sued?"

"Just a second." There was a series of clicks and pops on the other end of the line. Then Blakely was back. "International Consolidated Investments, Inc. The point of contact for the suit was a Hector Rodriguez in Virginia."

"Where in Virginia?"

"McClean. Does that mean anything to you?"

"Maybe."

"Well, I think I have some good news and bad news for you. Which do you want first?"

"You've solved the case?"

"Not exactly. But I think I know what's going on."

"What about the ticking clock? We haven't got that much time left."

"Not to worry. I'll bet you could not find anything that matched the countdown."

"That's right. Don't keep me in suspense. I'll take the good news first."

"The good news is that you don't have to worry about the case. It would be my guess that all of your records on the four are going to be seized and sealed by the FBI within a matter of hours. That will finish your involvement."

"That's going to leave an unsolved on my watch."

"It's going to leave nothing on your watch. It's going to be as if the situation never happened at all. Some federal man or woman in a black suit and white shirt will tell you that the case never existed."

"I wish all my cases were like that. What's the bad news?"

"It's going to cost the American taxpayer $1 million. Here's how I figure it. Our perp's husband was owed money by the CIA."

"The CIA? How did they get into this?"

"I'm betting that the perp's husband was a CIA agent. He was working for an import-export company, had a Cuban wife with close Cuban contacts – close enough to run arms to Castro and drugs from Castro."

"How do you know that?"

"First, all of the women are in their late 60s and early 70s and the records you have for them are sparse. That means the records of the first two were fakes, to be used as backup if someone is going to check on them. Even if they are real, the crimes are very old. Maybe they actually did run guns for Castro in the 1960s; that would even make them better agents. If they were working for the CIA – which I believe they were – the CIA would want to make sure that when Castro's people got into NCIC they would find the women were, to use the term your co-worker used, 'real bad dudes.' Same goes for our third perp, the one supposedly on trial in New York for three railroad boxcars of cocaine. That's a lot of cocaine for a 70-year-old woman to be pushing. I'd bet she's being run through the system to give her credibility."

"Those are all rather wild guesses."

"Really? Then why is our *non sequitur* suing a company that isn't even in Florida for a cat it probably doesn't have?"

"I don't know. Neither did the judge."

"That's right. That company is located just outside Langley, home of the CIA. I'll bet if you start looking at the company closely you'll find it doesn't really exist. It's a CIA front. For some reason, Mrs. Hendershoting feels that the CIA owes her and her three co-conspirators $1 million for something. She's asked for it and the CIA has said no. Then she sued for it, hopeful that the CIA would settle quietly rather than have one of its front operations exposed in Florida. That didn't work so the quartet took another step forward. They threatened to release something, maybe some documents they had hidden for just such a contingency. Whether they actually have such documents or not I do not know, but they had to draw attention to themselves in such a way that the CIA would get the message that they were serious."

"Why the garbage dump?"

"First, because it's not illegal to steal from the dump. It's just embarrassing. They knew they would be arrested. They wanted to be. So they made it look like they knew exactly where something was and they were extracting it. After all, they were not dressed for digging. The shovels wouldn't have done them any good and the arthroscopic equipment was a hint that they knew just about where to look for whatever it was they were supposed to have. Second, they knew that they would be arrested by a sheriff, not a policeman. Sheriff's departments are more loosely run than police departments. Your computers are not as good or as fast as the big city ones and you are a lot more lax in how you treat your prisoners. You don't throw them in a jail cell and throw away the key. They knew they were only going to be in jail for few hours, so why get tossed in with the general population? They got arrested, their names hit the NCIC, the FBI got the tip and contacted the CIA. Thirteen seconds later you didn't have a case. It just kind of disappeared."

"What makes you think the CIA is going to pay?"

"They're going to have to. They can't have four ex-agents running all over Florida getting arrested so they can spill whatever beans they know to some newspaper. No, the CIA will pay and that will be the end of the story."

"You seem pretty sure of yourself."

"Actually this was an easy case. Once the feds showed up I could pretty much say anything I wanted. They're not going to tell you anything. But, frankly, I think I've hit the nail on the head."

"Well, it's one hell of a story. But there are some loose ends. What about the clock running backwards? What about the dosing wires?"

"Ah, the clock! That was a bit tricky. I cheated a bit there. I had you looking for everything that I could think of off the top of my head. But after I thought about it and the pieces started to fit, I did some checking on my own. What, I asked myself, is going to happen in about 120 hours? You reached me at 1 p.m. Alaska Time on Thursday which means you were talking to me at 5 p.m. Florida time. So the 121 hours would have ended Monday in the early afternoon here in Alaska and the end of the afternoon on the East Coast. On a hunch I called the Alaska Congressional Office and asked for a complete list of meetings that were to take place on Monday afternoon. One of them was a closed-door meeting of the joint House-Senate Intelligence Committee. That's when the pieces started falling into place. The ticking clock was just a stark reminder to the CIA that, excuse the pun, 'the clock was ticking' on their demands. The CIA apparently took that seriously."

"And the dosing rods?"

"Who knows? I figure they took those along to confuse the Sheriff's department. Everything else fit with a treasure hunt in the garbage. The dosing rods were just to confuse the issue, stall for time."

"So this was nothing more than a shakedown by four old women against the elite East Coast corporate structure?"

"You sound like you went to Berkley."

"Class of 72."

"You go, girl. And tell your commissioner to tell my commissioner that I should have another two days off with pay for working on my holiday."

THE MATTER OF THE PENNY-ANTE KLEPTOMANIAC

Captain Heinz Noonan, the "Bearded Holmes" of the Sandersonville Police Department, was deeply engrossed in the ongoing drama of a personal relationship –with his goldfish, Chester.

The two were best of friends.

At feeding time.

It was feeding time and the "Bearded Holmes" was nose-to-snout with only a sheet of glass between the two. One was ignoring the particles of fish food trickling down from above and the other was wondering why the fish food was *not* drifting down on the inside of the fish tank. It was only when one of the particles landed on Noonan's nose did he realize he had been feeding the floorboards of his office and not Chester. With a flick of his tail, Chester was gone in a flight of indignation.

"Cockroaches will love the fish food," yelled Harriet from across the room. Harriet was Noonan's no-nonsense administrative assistant, mother confessor and paperwork tyrant. Without her the Detectives – both the office of that name and the denizens therein – would be a mob rather than a cohesive office where something actually got done.

"How'd you know I missed again?" snapped Noonan.

"Simple," she replied. "It's 10 a.m. on a Monday, Wednesday or Friday and that's feeding time for Chester and every feeding time for Chester starts with fish food for the cockroaches. I know that even though my back is turned."

Noonan peered over the top of Chester's tank and, just as she had stated, her back was turned.

"This is outrageous," he started to say.

"Yeah," Harriet said as she turned around, "but the cockroaches love it! Before you get snippy, there's a call on Line One. It's one of your specialty calls."

"Captain Noonan."

"This is Javier de la Vega from Morrison City. I'm told you can solve unusual crimes."

"It's been said but I've been lucky."

"This is an odd one."

"If you're calling me, it's odd. What do you have?"

"We have a penny-ante kleptomaniac. But it is not what is being stolen that is bothering us. It's where the thievery has been committed."

"OK. Where have the thefts been taking place?"

"In locked rooms within secure vaults in a passkey protected building."

Javier de la Vega did not look like a Javier de la Vega was

supposed to look. He looked Irish. Right down to the red hair and freckles.

"This will be terribly racist," Noonan began but Vega finished his sentence.

". . . but you don't look like a d*e la Vega*."

"You said it, I didn't."

Vega laughed. "There's an old joke in Boston. A minister asks a child if she is a Steinberg and she says 'Yes.' The minister asks if her father is Rabbi Steinberg and she says 'yes.' Then he asks if her mother is Jewish and the child says 'yes.' Then why, the minister asks why does the child think she's Irish? The child replies she must be Irish because she was born in Boston."

"Let me guess, you're Irish."

"Mother was. My father was kindof/sortof Spanish."

"What is kindof/sortof?"

"This is more ethnic that I wanted to get but let's finish it."

"If that was a pun on the Finns I am not impressed."

"It wasn't but you're quick. I get asked about my name and heritage a lot because I look Irish with a Spanish name. Do you know why they call Italians wops?"

"Do I want to know?"

"For the story of my name, yes."

"OK, why?"

"Because when the Italian immigrants came through Ellis Island many of them had no identification. So the United States Immigration Service – or whatever it was called in the days – filled out paperwork for them in English. Then the Immigration Service agents stamped WOP on the forms, WOP for *With Out Papers*."

"And this is important because . ." Noonan let the question hang.

"Because my grandfather from Spain, who did not speak English, said, in Spanish that he came from the meadowlands, the low lands, *de la vega*. It was easier for the Immigration Agent to list him as *de la vega* than my grandfather's official six names most upper class Spaniards had at that time."

"Good enough for me," Noonan said. "But it is neither here nor there when it comes to this case."

"Actually," de la Vega noted, "it is at the heart of the case. My grandfather married well – which was easy in the days because he came with money – and had six children. They married well and we ended up with an extended family of 39. That is, there are 39 of us still living. We are all partners in the same family company. And referring the ancestral discussion we just had, we are the ethnic rainbow of America: Spanish, Italian, Jewish, Muslim, Mexican, African and we even have a woman from Iceland in the mix."

"What does the company do?"

"It's an odd company for America. It does not have a central purpose, like selling computers or dentistry. My grandfather wanted everyone to 'do their own thing' – he was a very 1960s kind of guy when he died – and left shares of stock in the company he founded to his six children and grandchildren to do what they wanted. But none of his blood descendants could sell their stock."

"So you are one big happy family."

"Uh, yes. Sort of."

"In my world," Noonan said. "That's a very big *no*."

"Well, we have our disagreements. Each of the six families has an equal share in the company and each of the six families went their own way. Then their kids went their own way with the shares they had and today we've got a company that is, shall we say, eclectic. Our services include guitar construction, software consultants, book and music publishing, shoe repair some teachers, two doctors and a lawyer."

"All under the same roof?"

"The traditional business, yes. But the teachers, doctors and the lawyer have offices of their own outside of the building."

"The building being the one where the kleptomania is striking."

"Correct."

"None of those professions sound like they need a locked vault much less a secure room."

"They don't. My grandfather made his money in diamonds and precious gems. That's the source of the wealth. The diamonds are in a secure vault in the locked room with a passkey protected portion of the business."

Noonan shook his head. "I'm trying to see what the problem is. None of the diamonds are missing so there's been no theft."

"Yet. We are concerned because what has been stolen was specially meant to attract our attention."

"Meaning?" ask Noonan.

"Three weeks ago a desk blotter was stolen. Two weeks ago it was the carafe from the coffee maker. Last week paper tray for the copier."

"These items were in the vault?"

"No, the locked room where the vault is located."

"Do you have security cameras in the locked room?"

"We have one over the door outside the room but no camera in the room. Lots of the family go in and out of that room all the time. We're not concerned with what goes in the room, just what comes out. I've looked over the tapes for the last three weeks and there is nothing suspicious coming out."

"But no camera inside the room?"

"There has never been a reason no reason to have one in the room. It's a small room with just a desk and office material."

"What's the desk used for?"

"Anyone who has to work in the room opens their vault drawer and takes out of they need. If they have to work in a secure location, they use the desk. Then they lock up and leave. You see, the vault has more than diamonds. It has all of the documents for all of the businesses, software designs, guitar wood that has to stay at a certain temperature, personal drawers for each family members."

"How big are the diamond drawers?"

"Small. Diamonds are not that large. Just large enough for the diamonds in their envelopes. We're talking about a bank of drawers that are two inches high, two feet wide and ten drawers high."

"None of the diamonds are missing?"

"Not yet."

"But you believe that diamonds are about to be stolen?"

"We're being careful."

Noonan leaned back in his chair. "I'm going to have to think about this for a while. But I am going to need some more information."

"Wait a second," *de la Vega* said, "Let me write this down."

"I need to know how many personal locked drawers there are in the entire vault including the diamonds. What the largest drawer and the smallest? Is there an actual safe, I mean one with tumblers, in the vault? How many people have used the vault in the last three weeks and how many were repeat visits? Has there been any discussion about changing the character of the company lately and if so, what is the vote? How many diamonds did your grandfather leave the company and how many do you have now? When was the last time the vault door combination was changed? Who changed it? Does the vault have any other type of security, like a motion or heat detector? That will do it for the moment."

"I can answer some of those questions now."

"No, I want all the answers together. How long do you think it will take to get the answers?"

"A day or so."

"Fine. I'll expect to hear from you, say, in two days. Oh, one more thing. How much does everyone in the extended family know about diamonds? Are any members of the family jewelers or appraisers of gems or antiques?"

"I'll get you what I can."

Three days later *de la Vega* was back like a bad penny.

"OK, I have all of the information you wanted."

"Shoot."

"No one in the family is a jeweler or appraiser per se. I'm a broker and I have handled the sale of gems, antiques and historic items but I never handled the actual items. I just dealt with their paper, the Provenance of the objects. There are 60 personal locked drawers, some members of the family have more than one. Of them, 11 are empty in the sense that no one is using them. They may have been used in the past but are not active in the sense that someone has placed anything in any of the 11 empty drawers. The other drawers vary in volume from the size of a file cabinet drawer to the diamond drawers which are two inches high, two feet wide and two feet deep. There are ten drawers of diamonds. There are two safes in the vault but they do not have tumblers. They have keys which are kept on pegs over the safe."

"Why do you have keys for a safe over the safe?"

"Sometimes we do business with outsiders. The meeting might last through lunch so we put all of the working material into the safe and lock the safe with the key. Then we take the key to lunch to show the client that the paperwork will be out be tampered with."

"I see. Go on."

"Over the last three weeks there have been 76 visits to the vault and of those, 15 people made three visits, 7 made two. The rest were single time visits. There are always discussions about changing the character of the company and all are serious. But the real problem is that selling diamonds is tricky. They do not have a firm market value like the price of oil or beef. Where, how and when you sell them has more to deal with their value than how many are on the market. Everyone is talking about selling but no one knows how to go about it without being skinned. My grandfather left six drawers of diamonds. The other four drawers are empty. All drawers are locked with double key entry. The vault door lock combination is changed every three months and the last it was changed was eight weeks ago. The combination is changed by an expert we hire and we always hire a different expert to change the code. Four of us are there when the code is changed. Then the code is passed out to the responsible members of the family."

"Responsible meaning?"

"Six copies are made, one for each of the families. The only people in those families who get the code are those who need it. No young children or people out of town."

"Security other than the door?"

"None."

"Do you want the good news or the bad news?"

"You've solved the crime?!"

"No. There is no crime here. Here's what I think is going on. There is a crisis brewing, what kind I cannot tell you. Since there have been three kleptomaniac thefts and there are 15 people who have made three visits, one of them is responsible for the thefts. There have been three thefts. I'm betting that the first one was to attract attention. The desk blotter did not get out the door so it is probably in an empty diamond drawer. It is flat and if you tried to bend it you would get particles of the blotter all over the floor. No one noticed any particles so the blotter was not bent."

"OK, I'll check."

"The second theft was the carafe from the coffee maker. The kleptomaniac could not have broken the carafe to get it because it would have left glass shards all over the floor. That would have attracted attention so the carafe is still in one piece. No one thought to check the empty drawers because, after all, it was just a carafe. I'm betting no one even thought to consider it missing."

"You are right. I have not checked the empty drawers. But why would someone want to steal a carafe and hide it?"

"The kleptomania theft was meant to attract attention, not to steal the carafe."

"Why would someone do that?"

"That, my dear *de la Vega*, is an interesting questions. My guess, somehow someone has been stealing diamonds. He, or she, has been taking them one at a time and selling them. No one is checking the diamonds on a regular basis so no one knows the diamonds are being smuggled out. I'm guessing that good diamonds are going out the door and cheap diamonds or even cut glass is being put in their place."

"How do you know that?"

"I don't. I'm guessing. I'm also guessing that someone other than the thief figured out what was happening. But the discoverer of the theft either did not know who was actually stealing the diamonds or the thief so close to the person who made the discovery he could not turn in the thief without blemishing himself or his family. So, instead of announcing the discovery, he began stealing meaningless objects to draw the attention of the family that something was amiss."

"Really?"

"Really. You didn't come here to get me to solve this non-crime. You wanted me to look at the facts and suggest a check of the entire vault, drawer by drawer. That would lead to the discovery of the blotter and carafe that no one cares is missing and the third object . . ."

"Paper tray."

"Yes, the paper tray. When all three objects show up in locked, empty drawers, someone is going to say, 'Hey, we should check the diamonds.' A diamond appraiser will be brought in and that's when the diamond thefts are going to be discovered.

Since no one can prove who took the diamonds, the family will simply file an insurance claim and that will be that."

"Then no one will ever know who took the diamonds." *de la Vega* said and was probably shaking his head though Noonan could not see it over the phone line.

But Noonan shook his head. "Are you familiar with the term *stalking horse*?"

"Can't say that I am."

"A century ago in Europe, when a hunter needed to sneak up on game, say deer, he walked behind a horse, a *stalking horse.* The deer saw the horse but did not recognize it as a threat. When the hunter behind the stalking horse got near enough for shot, he took it. The deer never saw the hunter coming."

"What does that have to do the missing diamonds?"

"You used me as your *stalking horse.* You're the alleged kleptomaniac. It took three subtle thefts to get your family to suggest going for a detective. You knew right where to come. Can I prove it? Nope. Do I want to? Nope. There's only been a crime when it's been reported and right now all that will happen is the insurance company will list the gems as missing. The assumption might even be the missing diamonds were never there in the first place, that your grandfather only said they were diamonds because he wanted everyone in the family to think they were rich. But it doesn't matter. The insurance company is going to pay and that will be that."

"But you think I am the kleptomaniac?"

"It doesn't matter. I'm a civil servant responding to an inquiry from the public. Unless a crime is reported no crime has been committed – and the discovery of a misplaced desk blotter, coffee maker carafe and paper tray do not even rise to the level of petty theft."

de la vega didn't say anything.

"You were kind of harsh on the boy, don't you think?" snapped Harriet from across the room.

"Maybe," replied Noonan. "I'm guessing it's his way of keeping his wife out of the slammer."

"You think his wife did it?"

"Don't know. Don't care. It's time to . . .

"Yeah, I know," shouted Harriet as she went for her third cup of the coffee of the morning. "Time to feed the cockroaches."

THE MATTER OF THE PHANTASMAGORIC HIGHBINDER

Captain Noonan, the "Bearded Holmes" of the Sandersonville Police Department, was speaking in a conspiratorial whisper when the call came in. He and Harriet were in cahoots as to how best to convince the scourge of their joint existence, Sandersonville Commissioner of Homeland Security Lizzard, to take an extended vacation. They had thought to create an office pool with the winner going to the Bahamas for the winter – and summer – but that was too obvious. They considered Las Vegas but neither wanted to bring the Commissioner joy, Bangor was too cold any time of year and Orlando too close. Barrow, Alaska, was a strong contender because it was as far as you could go from Sandersonville and still speak English.

The two were in a deep in devious mode when Harriet had to take a call on the office phone. Noonan was still pouring over slow-boat-to-China schedules to wherever they arrange for Lizzard to travel on vacation when Harriet handed him the phone.

"This is your kind of call."

Noonan took the phone. "Captain Noonan here. How can I help you?"

"This is Wang Feng Lee with the San Francisco Bay Chinatown Historic Manuscript Archives. We have a phantasmagoric highbinder who is appearing in our collections and no one believes us."

"I don't doubt that. I know the term *phantasmagoric* but I am unfamiliar with *highbinder*."

"That's because you're not from the West Coast. It's a San Francisco Bay term – historical term actually – for the Chinese Tong gangsters in the 1800s. The Tongs were gangs in San Francisco."

"That was a long time ago. Is there a specific reason you are using the term *highbinder*?"

"Because he appears on the security camera inside our vault just as if he stepped out of a time capsule. He's authentic right down to the queue and hatchet."

"How do you know you're not being fooled by some razzle-dazzle electronics?"

"Because the highbinder left behind an opium pipe in the vault. Our curator identified the opium as a 19th Century blend."

"You can probably buy that kind of opium if you know where to go."

"True. But can it set off a smoke alarm in a locked vault?"

"And," finished Noonan, "since nothing has been stolen there is no crime."

"The Bay City Police think we're crazy. The officer that took the report had a hard time keeping a straight face."

"I can believe it."

"But then someone at the security company talked to someone who talked to someone else and *poof* it was in a local tabloid and from there, well, you can imagine what happened next."

"Front cover in the supermarket tabloids. Since I cannot go to the San Francisco Bay Area, let me see what I can do from the other side of the country. First off, tell me about the San Francisco Bay Chinatown Historic Manuscript Archives."

"Do you know the difference between a museum and an archive?"

"Maybe. Tell me anyway."

"A museum is a building displaying historical items. An archive is a building that only houses paper. If you went to a museum you would see paintings and silverware, maybe a diorama of old San Francisco with a cable car in the background and manikins in period dress in the foreground. We are a manuscript archive. We have old letters, diaries, some manuscript, photographs, maybe some ration stamps and old identity cards. Generally speaking, we just have paper."

"Does the paper have any value? I mean in terms of cash."

"If you mean can you sell an old letter on Ebay, yes. But we are not talking even hundreds of dollars. We buy West Coast Chinese documents off Ebay but we're paying, at the most, a hundred dollars."

"What's the most valuable item in your collection?"

"We have some family histories from well-known 19th Century Chinese families but you'd have to know West Coast Chinese history to know who those people were. And the collectors who buy that kind of a collection are buying to give it to us."

"So there's no reason for anyone to want anything out of the collections for monetary gain?"

"I'd say not."

'Now let's talk about the highbinder and the opium pipe. Did the highbinder just stand and then disappear or did he walk around in the vault?"

"He just appeared. There was nothing dramatic about his appearance, like a flash of light or something like that. The vault is lighted 24 hours a day for the security camera to work. One moment the highbinder was not there the next moment he was. He had an opium pipe in his hand and he pointed at some boxes on a shelf. Then he set the pipe on the floor and was gone."

"So the highbinder didn't move around the vault?"

"No. He just stood there, pointed to some boxes on a shelf, put down the opium pipe and disappeared."

"Did the security camera pick up the pipe before the highbinder appeared? I mean, could the pipe have been on the floor before the highbinder appeared?"

"It could have been. The security cameras are trained on the collections, not the floor. They are primarily for fire and water problems, not people. I mean, who'd want to steal documents that have very little value?"

"Good point. Now, the highbinder pointed to some boxes on a shelf. Was that a single collection or does that shelf have many boxes for many people's letters, diaries, manuscripts, whatever?"

"Half of the shelf is for one collection, the *Fahn Quai.* It's an unusual collection. You see, *Fahn Quai* was the term the Tongs used to describe whites. It translates as 'foreign devil' or 'white devil.' That particular collection has documents relating to work of missionaries in Chinatown who were rescuing singsong girls from lives of prostitution. Sometimes the police would raid a brothel and the missionaries would parcel out young girls to families that would raise them."

"Does the collection have names, dates and other data like that?"

"Some. But most of the names are in Chinese and worthless today. I mean, if you think that someone wanted to make sure that no one knew their grandmother was a singsong girl, that's not likely. The singsong girls had names like Morning Dove, Rainbow and Sunshine. When they were freed they became June Morgan or Stephanie Albertson."

"How about the other collections on that shelf?"

"Some land titles from buildings that burned down in the San Francisco Earthquake and Fire, diaries of some Chinese servicemen during the Korean War, a few dozen identity cards from the Second World War and lots of letters."

"Were the letters all part of a single collection or were they acquired one at a time?"

"Both."

"How about the Korean War diaries. Anything special about them?"

"Several of them are unusual. They were by Chinese-American who had been taken prisoner of war by the Chinese. So here they were, Chinese-American soldier in a Prisoner of War camp being guarded by the Chinese. It was a strange ethnic mixing if you know what I mean."

"I can imagine."

"Now to the opium pipe. That pipe could have been on the floor for days, right?"

"Maybe not days but a day or two. We don't walk all the aisles between the collections every day. That aisle is not well used so, yes, the pipe could have been there for a few days. But the smoke alarm did go off until right after the highbinders set the pipe down."

"That leads to another set of questions. Tell me about the security arrangements for the vault."

"I may have mislead you by calling it a vault. You might think it is something like a bank vault that has a time lock and a dial. Ours is just a fireproof door with a key lock, nothing elaborate. Inside the vault we have a security camera and a smoke detector."

"And the lighting inside never goes off."

"Correct."

"I'm assuming that there is some recording mechanism for the security camera. Where are the tapes held?"

"In my office. The camera runs continuously so it's not as if we have a tape for June 1st and a tape for June 2nd."

"Who has a key to your office?"

"Oh, I'd say about five people. I do, my assistant does and the security company has three."

"And the smoke alarm?"

"It goes off when it goes off. There is no timer."

"Now, when the smoke alarm went off. What happened in sequence?"

"First, the fire department was notified. They notified me at home and I rushed down to the archive. Security had already let the fire department into the vault. We could still smell the opium. That's when we found the pipe."

"And then you found the footage of the highbinder?"

"When we looked at the security camera footage, yes."

"You said your assistant had a key. Where was he?"

"She's at a conference in Atlanta. I reached her by phone. She had her key with her."

"Now, the opium pipe. How do you know it is an antique?"

"It had better be. Opium has been illegal in California for a century."

"Then how do you know the opium is an old blend?"

"The chemistry department at the state college matched it a mixture from a century ago."

"Do you trust them?"

"They also serve the crime lab for the police, so, yes, I trust them."

"You said that you filed a police report. Why?"

"It's a requirement with the security company. If they respond to any kind of a call, the police are notified."

"Did the police find the highbinder?"

"Actually, yes. They looked at the security tape and found the phantasmagoric figure."

"What did they say?"

"They thought it was a joke."

"What do you think?"

"I think it's a prank. I don't know how it was done but I don't believe in ghosts."

"OK. I need you to do some research for me. Do you have a pen and paper?"

"Sure."

"OK. Did you or the security company smell burned opium when you opened the vault? Is the key to the vault generic in the sense that you could get duplicate keys made at a hardware store? Was there anything unique about the highbinder that proved he was a century old? Are there more than one Chinatowns in the Bay Area and if so, where? Does your document collection included diaries and letters from just the Bay Area and if not, where else do the documents come from? Is there a local acting guild and if so, is it doing a play that includes a highbinder? I'm sure I will have some other questions when you call back."

"I can give you some of those answers now."

"No. I want all the answers at the same time."

"You got it. I'll call back tomorrow morning."

"You mean afternoon. Your morning is my afternoon."

"I forgot you were on the East Coast."

It took two days for Wang Feng Lee to get back with Noonan.

"Any more highbinder specters?"

"No. Just the one. The good news is that the local newspapers thinks it's a prank so they won't print anything."

"You think it's a prank too, right?"

"I don't know what to think."

"That's a good way to start an investigation. Did you get the information I needed?"

"I got what you wanted but I don't know if it will help you. I got to the vault well after the fire department and the security company got there so I didn't smell anything. The security people said it smelled like burned spice. The fire department people just said it smelled like something burned. I wouldn't know what burned opium smelled like so that doesn't help you at all."

"OK."

"Yes, the key to the vault is generic. You could get a copy made at a hardware store and, I hate to say this, I leave my keys in my desk drawer. All days and sometimes all night. Anyone could have gotten the key and made a duplicate. That won't happen again."

"Go on."

"Highbinders did not change their style over the years. A highbinder in 1860 would like just like a highbinder in 1906. Look at any photograph of a highbinder and there is no way of knowing what year the photo was taken. They dressed in loose black shirts and trousers. They all had queues. So, no, there is nothing unique about the highbinder that would prove he was a century old. There were lots of Chinatowns in the Bay Area but with the exception of San Francisco, they were simply areas where the Chinese lived. Most were gone by the First World War. San Francisco's Chinatown has been there since the building of the railroad. We have diaries and letters from all over Bay Area and there is no local play that has a highbinder."

There was a long moment of silence. Finally Wang Feng Lee asked if he were still there.

"Yup. One last question. The Chinatowns in the Bay Area that disappeared. When did the last one go?"

"It's going now. Right here in town. There's a highway coming through."

"Any Chinese left in that area?"

"No. They are long gone."

"OK. Here's what I think is happening. First, having the phantasmagoric highbinder appear would be child's play. All someone had to do was get a duplicate of your key – which you said would not be hard – and then wait until the middle of the night. They would get into the vault with your key and do the disappearing and appearing."

"How would they do that?"

"There were probably two of them. One person to stop the security camera until the highbinder was in place. Then that person would turn the camera on. The highbinder would do his part, point to a box on a shelf and then the camera would be turned off. The highbinder would then drop the opium pipe and leave the vault."

"But the opium pipe . . ."

"Could have been bought from anywhere. That century-old opium was probably in the form of tar on the inside of the pipe. I found more than 30 antique opium pipes on EBay. You could probably get century old opium tar from any other pipe. Besides, your chemist did not say that the opium was 100 years old, only that it was a century old blend. That blend could have been concocted a week ago."

"OK. So the two people open the vault, do a little highbinder dance, leave the opium pipe and set some kind of a spice on fire to set off the fire alarm. Is that what you are saying?"

"That's what I think happened. They stopped the tape until the highbinder impersonator got into the vault. Then the camera turned on for five seconds, just enough time for the high binder to point to the shelf and drop the opium pipe. Then the camera was turned off."

"So that's why the highbinder appeared out of thin air and disappeared into thin air?""

"My guess, yes."

"Then they pair left the building."

"Yup."

"Why?"

"That is what I've been thinking about for two days. Since nothing came out of the vault, the only answer is that something went in. My bet is that someone put a document into one of the boxes on the shelf. My bet: it was in the box on land records. You said that there was a highway project in your city. Well, if an old land title was suddenly discovered, whoever is funding the highway would have to buy the property. They would probably have to move fast too. They would not slow down a $45 million project for a $100,000 piece of property."

"So you think it's a scam?"

"I don't know what it is. But my advice is to go through the manuscripts and documents regarding land title and see if a new document has been added. It won't be a San Francisco piece of property because I'll bet people have been looking at those documents for years. No, it will be small piece of property. Maybe a quarter share of lot where there was Chinese grocery store or something like that. Land records a century ago are not what they are today. If you don't find it, *someone* is going to hint at it in the newspaper. Better you find it."

"So someone is trying to scam the government?"

"That's my guess."

"I wouldn't think they'd have a Chinaman's chance . . ."

"You can say that! I can't."

THE MATTER OF THE COZENED GNOMES

Heinz Noonan, the "Bearded Holmes" of the Sandersonville Police Department was enjoying a pleasant evening on vacation in confines of the fine Merlot as he was dining on King Salmon at Munsey's Bear Camp on Uyak Bay. Uyak Bay was on the remote west side of Kodiak Island and the key word for Noonan was *remote* because it meant he was distant from his mother-in-law and in-laws in Anchorage as well as far as he could be from the politics of the Sandersonville Police Department as he could be and still speak English. Alas, he was still within the grasp of the treacherous beast of Satan which, at that very moment, was vibrating in his cargo pants' pocket. He did not have to look at the number on the face of the infernal instrument of mayhem to know it was his wife. She was off with his close friend, Robin Barefield, and fishing for King Salmon on the far side of Uyak Bay. Who else would call?

"Yes, dear," Noonan said lazily. "I hope you caught a nice fat one because I look forward to a fine king salmon repast this evening."

"Fine with me," said a strange voice. "But I'm more concerned with the theft of 150, two-foot high, garden gnomes that are turning up in vacant lots all over the city."

"Gnomes?"

"Yes, sir. You know, gnomes like the one in the advertising for that travel service on television."

"You mean garden gnomes, right?"

"Yes, sir."

"Well, first of all, who are you and how did you get my number?"

"First, I am Brando Tagaloalagi. I'm the Sheriff of Chillingworth County in Western Washington and Harriet will deny she gave me your number."

"I've never heard of any Harriet," snapped Noonan. "And I'll bet no one has ever asked you about your name."

"Samoan names are quite popular among Samoans."

Noonan snorted. "I'm sure they are. Are you a lot of Samoans in, where?, Chillingworth County?"

"There are now."

"Good answer. I was interested in the Brando name."

"My mother was an aspiring actress and fan of Marlin Brando."

"A good answer. Give you mother my best."

"She'll appreciate that. She manages the local youth theater here in Chillingworth."

"OK. Enough. What's the problem?"

"Well, I was told when it came to unusual . . ."

"Yes, yes, I know. The problem. I've got a glass of chilled wine and I'd like to get back to it."

"Not a problem. About a year ago there was a theft of a boxcar of garden gnomes. The gnomes are a foot-and-a-half high. They were taken out of a railway boxcar that was on a sidetrack. Someone snapped the lock on the box car and took every box of gnomes out."

"How many gnomes are we talking about?"

"Maybe 150. The shipping documents were scattered. That is, the company sending the gnomes knew 560 gnomes were sent west. Along the way boxes were taken off for delivery. To get an exact number the company would have had to contact every distributor who would have to contact every store where the gnomes were sold to get a total of the gnomes that were *not stolen.* It was not worth the gnome company's time to get a number. All it wanted was the police report for the insurance company. The company estimated 150 gnomes. That's the number I'm stuck with."

"150 gnomes?"

"Correct. If that was all, I wouldn't be calling you. The theft was about a year ago. 14 months, actually. But within the last month they have been appearing in vacant lots all over Chillingworth. We picked up about a dozen of them but they get replaced. So now we just leave them in place."

"Why would anyone want to steal a gnome let alone 150 of them and then leave a bunch of them all over town a year later?"

"That, sir, is why I'm calling you."

Noonan was silent for a moment. Then he said, "Tell you what. Call me back in an hour. Let me think about this for a while."

"Yes, sir."

"Heinz."

"Eh?"

"Heinz. I'm not a sir. If there's a crime and I'm duty, it's sir. There isn't a crime here."

"Heinz is fine with me if you call me Brando."

"Marlin won't work?"

"That's what my wife calls me when she's mad."

"Brando it is."

One of the blessings of the internet is its availability. Even at a remote lodge on the far side of Uyak Bay on Kodiak Island, an island most people in America do not even know exists. Noonan punched up garden gnomes on Wikipedia – and donated a sawbuck to the site because free information is not really free; someone is paying for it and if you use information from Wikipedia you should pay for it because there are people who cannot (or will not) – and did a quick read. Which was possible because there was not much he didn't know.

Garden gnomes were the 21st Century's Priapus, the Roman God of fertility, horticulture and viticulture. Just a glance at Priapus made it clear why he was god of fertility and, as Noonan was a wine connoisseur, he was familiar with viticulture. Small stone statues of Priapus with a sickle were common in Roman gardens. During the Renaissance Priapus became grotesque and were painted with wild, contrasting colors. Three hundred years later, in Germany, the evolving, grotesque Priapus were transformed into dwarfs or the legendary "little folk" of the region. Then, as with all things saleable, they were mass produced. In this century, Noonan discovered, the gnomes for sale usually had a red phrygian cap – he hit the link to phrygian for a definition – and sometimes have pipes. Pipes as what one uses with tobacco.

The only reference to the massive use of gnomes, other than for advertising, was a reference to a 2014 election in Austria where a minor party, the Social Democratic Party of Austria (DPO), used them as advertising. Dubbing them "coolmen," the party had traditional performed so poorly the press labeled them "political dwarfs." Just as Andrew Jackson had adopted the jackass as the symbol for the Democratic Party in America in the previous century, the DPO adopted the gnome. Then they placed more than 20,000 posters with gnomes and party slogan along the roadways. When more than 400 of the posters were stolen, the thefts (along with news anchors' laughter) were reported around the world.

When Tagaloalagi aka Brando called back, Noonan had a short list of questions. "OK, I've got a list of questions for you. Call me back when you have the answer to all of them. Ready,"

"Shoot, Luke."

"Luke?

"I'm in Eastern Washington. Cowboy country."

"OK, here we go. Why was the boxcar sitting at the siding? Was that on purpose or by accident? How long had it been sitting there? How was the theft discovered? Was it well known the gnomes were in the boxcar? How heavy were the boxes with the gnomes? Did any of the boxes ever show up? Are there any cults in the area? Have there been any increases in traffic violations in Chillingworth County since the gnomes were stolen? How many gnomes appeared in the vacant lots. Where were the vacant lots located? Were the gnomes you picked up dusted for fingerprints? That's all I can think about right now. I might have some more questions later."

"I'll see what I can do."

"Great. Just don't call at dinner time. Alaska time."

Four hours later, after Alaska dinner time, Brando was back on the phone. "Here's what I've got for you. In order. The boxcar had been there for two days. Chillingworth is a minor transportation hub for Western Washington so being on a railroad sideline for two days is not unusual. Everyone knew of the gnomes in the boxcar. It was in the newspapers as one of those humorous sidebars. About how Chillingworth was so small dwarfs were immigrating. The theft was discovered when the boxcar was visually inspected, an inspection required by regulation. The gnomes are four to a box and the boxes weigh 20 pounds. No gnome boxes have shown up. We don't have any cults, as in religious, in the area. The closest thing we have is a white nationalist separatist anti-immigrant/black/Samoan wacko group in the backcountry. There may be a dozen of them, maybe. We're a small community so we know who they are. And we don't care. Odd you show ask it, there has been an increase in traffic tickets. Parking tickets, not speeding tickets. You really have to be speeding in Chillingworth County to get a ticket. Parking tickets; a dime a dozen. Guessing you were going to ask, I did check the names of the offenders. A smattering of residents, a few scofflaws, and, surprisingly, a few of the white nationalist separatist anti-immigrant/black/Samoan wacko group. Yes, I know what you are going to ask next, most of those tickets were downtown. Not in residential areas or where the gnomes were found."

"You are one step ahead of me," Noonan said. "You're in the right profession to be forward thinking."

"Thanks. A total of 17 gnomes have been picked up and we are pretty sure another dozen were picked up by local residents. You know, finders-keepers. All were dusted. No prints. No markings or smudges. Like they were right out of the box. There are 20 gnomes out there now. Half of them are in the downtown area, the others are in some residential areas."

"Those gnomes in the residential areas, are they clustered in one area or several?"

"Three, if the number means anything."

"Any of the ones downtown area within sight of a grocery store, post office, federal building police station or the courthouse?"

"Heinz, everything in Chillingworth is within sight of the grocery store, post office, federal building police station or the courthouse?"

"Any special legal cases being heard in town?"

"Nope. The usual. Traffic tickets, shoplifting, small claims. Nothing big."

"Humm, I'm hoping you can live with a guess and not a solid answer."

"I'll take what I can get."

"This is just a guess, now. I'm betting there is a big legal case coming. And coming soon. A federal one. But it will be a lot of much ado about nothing. The kind of a case people laugh about."

"How do you know that?"

"Just a hunch. I think your white nationalist separatist anti-immigrant/black/Samoan wacko group in the backcountry –

your words – were the ones who stole the gnomes in the first place. I'm betting one of the members works for the railroad in some capacity so he would know where the boxcar was located. He and his buddies broke into the boxcar and took the gnomes as a political statement against immigrants. It was a publicity stunt that went nowhere."

"Good guess and likely true. But why are the gnomes appearing all over town?"

"I'll get to that. I'm guessing the gnomes were used by the cult as targets. They had failed at publicity and could not afford to be caught with the gnomes. So they began using them as targets."

"But the ones we picked up were complete, not shot-up."

"Correct. The cult didn't shoot all of them. As they were shooting up the gnomes, somehow, they got the word they were being investigated by the feds. If the investigation had been by the police or sheriff, the news would have been all over town. Chillingworth is that kind of community, it's it?"

"You got that one right."

"So, I'm betting the feds are involved. The feds are quiet sorts. But somehow the cult knew there was an investigation underway and suspected there was a mole. The way to remind the mole to keep his mouth shut was to put up gnomes around town, just like the ones they were shooting to pieces, in areas where the suspected mole lived and shopped. I'll bet the gnomes are in the residential area where the railroad worker lives, the one who tipped the cult as to the location of the boxcar. If they are in more than one area, then your white nationalist separatist anti-immigrant/black/Samoan wacko group suspects more than one person."

"That's quite a leap of logic. What do you think the feds are investigating?"

"I call them 'laughing indictments.' They are designed to make people look foolish rather than charge them with serious crimes. It will be something minor, like destruction of railroad property for the lock on the box car. Something to drag people into court and get laughs on the local news and in the newspaper."

"Why not the stealing of the gnomes?"

"No need. The gnomes are worth about $5 each. Wholesale. So 150 are $750, a pittance. My bet, the feds are going to threaten your railroad worker with breaking and entering, theft, white nationalist separatist anti-immigrant/black/Samoan wacko group in the backcountry trespassing on railroad property which is a violation of interstate commerce, littering, loitering and some other crimes. Or, they will say, you can plead down to breaking the padlock on the box car."

"I'd take that deal."

"So will your railroad worker. What the feds want to do is embarrass the cult, get the community laughing at them. There's great power in laughter. They don't want to spend $100,000 to get a conviction for stealing $750 worth of plaster and paint."

"Good thought. I'll keep you informed."

"NOT while I'm on vacation. I can live with the suspense."

Three days later, in the Kodiak Airport, the fiend of the underworld vibrated in his pocket. This time he looked the incoming call. "Drat!" he mumbled to himself, "the police department. What disaster am I going to be sucked into just as I coming home from vacation."

"Let me guess, Harriett. There's a national emergency in Sandersonville."

"Not quite," Harriett's voice said reaching across time and space. "You got a package from a Samoan in Chillingworth, Washington. I'm betting you solved the gnome mystery up there. Since I haven't heard from you, I'm guessing gnome news is good news."

"Very funny, Harriett, very funny. Did you search the internet for that one?"

"Wasn't hard. Gnome wasn't built in a day. Gnome home because your vacation's over."

"Enough of the gnome jokes. What was in the package."

"A gnome. What did you think was in the box?"

"No note?"

"Yeah, from a Brando with a Samoan name. Brando?"

"His mother is an old movie fan. What does the note say?"

"It reads 'No Place like Gnome. An Alaskan joke. You were right. Sentenced to 10 hours of community service. Here's one of the evidence gnomes. Enjoy.'"

"How nice."

"You're expected back on Monday. Gnome excuses."

Before Noonan could respond, the beast of Satan went silent. No dead because, as is well known, evil never sleeps.

THE MATTER OF THE FATTENING IGLOOS

Captain Heinz Noonan, the "Bearded Holmes" of the Sandersonville Police Department, was reading the travel section of the *Anchorage Daily Journal* and day dreaming of his upcoming trip to Alaska. The dreaming was not so much of the northland as it was of the king salmon he expected to catch – the daily limit each day he was in the North – and the spread of salmon dishes he expected to consume. Because his wife was Alaskan, she was tired of salmon in every concoction known and preferred chicken. Noonan was not so cursed and looked forward to salmon in any recipe.

He was contemplating the taste of a curry salmon roast when the phone on his desk – not the electronic beast of his jacket pocket – jangled. It did not have a visual indicator as to who was calling so he had to be polite.

"Captian Noonan. Can I help you?"

"Shore can, ol' buddy," said a voice that was Yankee trying to be Southern. "I got myself an igloo what's been picking up weight as she goes along. Gotta bill here I don' wanna pay."

"Really? Who are you, sir?"

"Festus Theobold. Of Balt-eh-more, Mar-land. I was told you is the kind of a guy who can solve this kinda problem."

"Well, Mr. Theobald."

"Bold. Bold like a knight shinging armor."

"Yes, Mr. Theobold," Noonan accented the "a" in the name. "You said an igloo. I assume you mean a cargo igloo and not an ice igloo."

"Got it, boy. Ain' no reason to have an ice igloo in these parts, if you know what ah mean. Yup, a plastic igloo. Square on the bottom and rounded on top, just like an Eskimo igloo."

"You have an igloo that's gaining weight?"

"Yes siree bob cat. I put it on the plane in Memphis at 125 pounds and it comes off the cargo plane in Sandersonville at 225. Picked up a 100 pounds along the way."

"You mean someone opened it up and put in an extra hundred pounds of something?"

"Got a seal on it. That is, it's enclosed with a fed lock. Airline folks put it on in Memphis and it's just as good as the moment it was latched. Ain' been opened. But it's 100 pounds heavier and I'll be damned if I'm gonna pay for some airline's jockey putting some stuff in and sticking me with the bill."

"This is the third time this has happened in the last month," Colonel Sanders of the Air National Guard told Noonan when he arrived at the Sandersonville cargo terminal. "No relation," Sanders said as it was clear Noonan was about to ask of his lineage. "He's from Kentucky; we're out of Dee-troit." He extended the "D" of "Detroit" as if it were a cattle call.

"Let me make sure I understand what the problem is," Noonan asked. "You have igloos that are getting loaded onto planes and they are picking up weight along the way. They start at, say, 100 pounds, and are unloaded at 150 pounds."

"That's a simple way of saying it. It's more complicated than that. Cargo is not like passengers. Passengers get onboard in Sandersonville and make Denver in one hop. That's because passengers breathe and buy liquor. The airlines want them moving as fast as possible. Cargo is different. It goes when it most efficient and profitable."

"In other words, cargo may or may not go on the next available flight."

"Cargo rarely goes on passenger flights. Except for mail, organs and real expensive stuff like Certificates of Deposit, $5,000 a bottle Scotch and furs. It usually goes by cargo plane. A plane could arrive in 10 minutes or not until the next day. The cargo could go through Atlanta on its way to Denver or through New York or New Jersey. It goes when it goes. No one complains. There's an old Alaskan cargo expression, 'cargo don't talk back.'"

"All right. So it goes when it goes. I'm assuming you weigh it when it comes in."

"That is correct. We need to know how heavy it is. That's because we have to charge the sender by the pound and we need to pack the plane so it is balanced. We cannot assume two packages of the same size have the same weight."

"If you weighed the igloos when they went onboard, why did you weight them when they came off the plane?"

"Security. Double-checking our system. It's not done on a regular basis. Randomly. We need to make sure our equipment is working and our staff on the ball."

"So how many igloos were overweight?"

"Three we've caught."

"Over the last, what, three months? Six months?"

"Weeks. Three weeks. Nothing was out of the ordinary until three weeks ago. Suddenly we've got three overweight. A bit over the weight variance. 8%, our standard."

"You think someone is trying to chisel on the weight?"

"Could be. Double the weight is double the price. If someone can send 150 pounds of igloo for 75 pounds there's a savings in their pocket. Multiply by ten packages and half your shipment is flying free."

"I must be missing something, Colonel."

"Sanders. Not the Kentucky Sanders, the Deee-troit Sanders."

"Yes sir. I am assuming when someone ships an igloo it is weighed when it comes in the cargo by door."

"That's correct."

"So the shipper is paying the correct amount."

"Yes, at that moment."

"But once the shipper leaves and the igloo gains weight, isn't that the problem of the air carrier, not the shipper?"

"We don't believe so. If the igloo is weighed when it comes off the plane and it weighs more, the assumption is that the initial weight was in error. The shipper is then billed for the exit weight – we call it the *exit weight* – not the entrance weight."

"But how the can igloo gain weight in your care?"

"We don't know. We just know that it does and we charge accordingly."

"I've got a cousin who can help you solve this," said Harriet, Noonan's Administrative Assistant in the Detective Office, as she lathered peanut butter on her bagel.

"Are you really going to eat *that*?" Noonan said when she topped the peanut butter with blackberry jelly.

"Yeah. What's it to you?" She took a bite. "My cousin Samantha has a scale that lies."

"What do you mean, lies?"

"Lies, you know. Lies. Doesn't reveal the truth. She's got a scale that says she's 120 even when she's not."

"You mean she weighs 140 and the scale still says she weighs 120."

"Try 160. It's from some kind of a self-esteem store. She wants to be 120. The scale says she's 120. She feel good about herself."

"But she weighs 160," snapped Noonan.

"In her mind," retorted Harriet, "she's 120. It makes her feel good. She's a better person. Has better Karma."

"That's garbage," snapped the detective.

"Maybe," said Harried. "But she feels good to be herself at 120 pounds." Harriet nibbled at her bagel. "How do you know the scale at the Sandersonville Airport is correct?"

"We did some test weights. It's accurate within a degree of error."

"Did the igloos that were overweight all come from the same airport?"

"Nope."

"Did the same cargo crews handle the outgoing igloos?"

"Nope."

"What did the owners of the igloo say when they found out their igloos were going to be charged more because of the weight?"

"They don't know. Probably still don't. These are large shippers. A certain amount of adjustment is expected. The number of overweight igloos are so small they do not warrant an investigation. When a company is shipping 60,000 pounds a month, a few hundred pounds over on some igloos is not worth their time to investigate."

"So someone's getting away with poundage theft."

"A better question is why?"

"Why don't you ask the Sandersonville Chief of Detectives? He's a crackerjack at solving those kind of inane questions."

Planes, as Noonan knew, routinely violate the laws of common sense. This is to say, what is reality to pilots takes some explaining to non-aviators. For instance, every pilot knows a plane becomes lighter the farther it flies. To non-aviators this is a *non sequitur.* How can a plane lose weight by flying? A plane is, after all, a plane and it is the same plane on the ground as it is in the air. This is only half-true. A plane on the ground is heavier than a plane in the air because a plane on the ground is loaded with fuel. As the plane flies, fuel is burned and the plane becomes lighter. This is an important bit of knowledge for seasoned pilots – particularly bush pilots in Alaska – because it means they can take off cautiously overloaded and when they reach a mountain range hours later the plane will weigh less so it can easily leap over the mountain tops.

But this bit of trivia did Noonan no good because it was weight being lost, not being gained. Logically, if an igloo weighed 100 pounds when checked in and 150 pounds when checked out, it must have gained 50 pounds somewhere along the way. This, of course, assumes the scales at both ends of the journey were accurate. In this he was sure because both scales were frequently checked by the United States Department of Weights and Measures. Even if the inspectors were a bit off, 50 pounds off was a bit much.

Since the igloos were sealed – a pun which Noonan appreciated since his wife was an Alaskan – something could not have been inserted. If it had been, the shipper would have reported it. Tossing an extra 50 pounds on top of the igloo was not reasonable because the extra 50-pound object would have been spotted by the person picking up the package. Igloos were a standard size and weight so putting something under the igloo when it was weighed was not a possibity either. Again, if there had been 50 pounds of something under the igloo it would have been spotted by the person picking up the igloo.

So how had the igloo gained weight?

On a hunch Noonan went back to the Sandersonville Airport. Colonel Sanders was still there – not of Kentucky but Deee-troit as he reminded Noonan again.

"Colonel," Noonan asked. "Are other airports having this problem?"

"Igloos with too much weight? Yes, if you mean a variance of up to 8%. Above that, rarely. We're regulated by every one of the alphabet soup agencies, state and federal. See, technically, we are an oddity. We are within a state but are not state property but cargo leaves here into the state so we are regulated by the state.

We handle cargo from overseas so the feds are involved but only as far as the front door. Then the cargo falls under state regulation."

"And you have to open your books to both the state and feds."

"That's right."

"Is this the only cargo facility with an overweight problem?"

"I haven't heard any other airport cargo facility has this problem." He quickly added, "Not that it is a *problem*, you understand. It's probably a paperwork error. And the weight is too small for us to worry about it. We handle tons of cargo so a few hundred pounds of error is not even peanuts."

"How can a 50% increase in weight be a paperwork error?"

"What else can it be? The scales are regularly checked at both ends of the journey. The igloos are sealed so nothing can go into it. There are lots of sizes of igloos but all of the sizes are the same weight. If there was something extra on top of the igloo or underneath the consignment drivers would report it. No, it has to be a paperwork error."

Noonan didn't say anything for a moment. "Do you mind if I look around?"

"You want to see the scales?"

"Sure. And take a look-see."

"Be my guest."

Noonan spent the next hour walking through the cargo warehouse. Though Sandersonville was not a large city there was an amazing amount of cargo. Much of it was pass-through. Noonan discovered that by reading the cargo labels. Igloos, crates and packages were coming from into the warehouse from all over the United States and then being shipped out to other cities on the North Carolina coastline. There was shelving for the smaller packages and crates while there were igloos on pallets on the main floor.

"What happens when you get more igloos then you have square footage in the warehouse?"

"It doesn't happen that often," a forklift operator told Noonan. "When it does we have extra space in a hangar near the runway."

"When igloos comes out of the warehouse, are they still weighed here in this warehouse?"

"Everything coming in or going out is weighed in this warehouse. The hangar is just a holding facility. The shippers still have to come here to check their cargo in or get it out."

"Any unusual cargo in or out over the past couple of months?"

"Nothing coming into Sandersonville is usual by your definition. We had an elephant once, for instance."

"An elephant?"

"Right. It came under its own power, if you know what I mean. Then it went out by air cargo on a trip to schools along the coast. To show kids there really were elephants. But it came in as cargo and went out as cargo. At least that was how it was charged."

"Any new clients in the past few months?"

"Same old same old. A few new ones. This is construction season so we're getting a lot of building material. A lot of tourism cargo is coming in, pretty much the same mix as last year at this time.

"Cargo ever get lost?"

"Lost? Sure. But not lost and never found. Small things get shuffled around a lot in here to make room for larger items. We get all sizes of things in here: flat, round, heavy, light, and bulky. We get steel rods that are long and, well, round. Then there are cases of meat that are in refrigerated containers and exotic ice creams that are in freezers. We get everything here."

"Did you find anything?" asked Colonel Sanders when Noonan came back to the front of the warehouse.

"Not really. Just a few more questions. The cargo that was overweight. Was all of the overweight cargo to the same shipper?"

"Not the ones we caught. Three different shippers."

"Were all of the overweight items igloos?"

"Yes."

"Were the overweight igloos all picked up by the same truck drivers?"

"That I could not tell you. We're only concerned with the cargo inside our doors. As long as the truck drivers have the proper paperwork they can have the cargo."

When Noonan got back to the office he pulled Lt. Weasel into a conference. "You have clothes other than your uniform?"

"Some jeans and T-shirts."

"How about a work shirt?"

"Never needed one."

"You do now."

Harriet spent the next morning whining about how three of the detectives had not made it into the office yet and here it was almost 11 a.m. Noonan kind of grunted and went back to his Jumble. By noon Harriet was beside herself.

"Did you give Weasel and the others the day off?"

"Who me?"

"Yes, you! If they get a day off, so do I!"

"As far as I know they're working."

"Is this another of those undercover jobs?"

"I'm not sure," Noonan said as Weasel and the three detectives came in. Weasel was smiling a cop smile: just a hint of one end of his lips twitching up.

"You were right, chief." Weasel said. "I can't tell you what they were smuggling but they were caught at it. It was a good idea to get the feds involved. We could only go as far as the check-in counter. The feds could go all the way in."

"What did they find?" Noonan asked.

"Beats the bejeezus out of me. You know the feds. They don't tell anyone anything."

Harriet was splitting a blouse seam. "OK, what's been going on?"

Weasel cut in before Noonan could speak. "Remember the overweight igloo problem?"

"OK," snapped Harriet. "What does it have to do with you and the rest of the staff getting the morning off and leaving me here with work to do?"

"We weren't taking the morning off. We were staking out the cargo warehouse. See, the extra weight wasn't in the igloos, on the igloos or under the igloos."

"Well, if the igloos was overweight. Where else could it be?"

"That's the brilliance of the scheme," said Weasel with too much excitement for a police officer. "The cargo workmen were smuggling stuff out of the warehouse. How it got in we do not know. What it was we do not know. But we do know how it was being smuggled out. It was in the pallets, the wooden frames under the igloo."

"What?"

"See, let's say the warehouseman wanted to smuggle 100 pounds of something out the warehouse. They had to account for the weight so what they did was put the smuggled items inside the frame of the pallet and then put an igloo on top. Then they loaded the pallet and frame onto the scale. The weight was recorded and then the igloo and the pallet with the smuggled goods was loaded onto a truck. The truck drives away and that's that. The shipper has so many tons of cargo coming in a few hundred extra pounds won't make any difference. A weight discrepancy will only be discovered in an audit of the cargo warehouse and by then the pallet is long gone."

"So the shipper has been getting the smuggled goods? That should be easy to prove."

"No," said Weasel. "The captain figured the shipper was *not* getting the smuggled goods. The truck drivers were. They were delivering the igloos and pulling the goods out from inside the pallets. The shippers never knew they were being used. Slipping the smuggled goods inside the pallets took seconds. The igloos covered up the goods in the pallet on the weighing machine and by the time the loaded pallets got to the shipper, the goods were gone."

"Pretty slick," said Harriet. She turned to Noonan. "Pretty clever on your part."

"No, on your Cousin Samantha's part. I liked your story. No matter how much she weighed the scales read the same. The weight varied but the scales did not. But what if it were reversed, the scales varied but the weight did not? At the scales the weight of igloos varied but its contents did not. The extra weight was not in the igloo; it was under the igloo."

"Those guys might have been smuggling for years. But they made a mistake with one pallet. That tripped them up."

"It's the little things that trip you up," Noonan said.

"Well, if that's the case, how about a *little thing* like half-day off for me to do some undercover work down at the beach?"